"I Need Someone—
You, Specifically—To Pose As
My Fiancée."

"Your what?" she gasped, shooting to her feet. "Are you crazy? That's just ridiculous. We don't even know one another."

"Ah, but we do."

He crossed the room in a few long strides, coming to a halt directly in front of her. The light scent she wore, something floral and innocent and totally at odds with the sensual creature he knew lingered under her proper exterior, wafted on the air between them. Will lifted his hand and traced one finger along the enticing fullness of her lower lip.

"Let me enlighten you."

He didn't give her so much as a split second to react. He closed the short distance between her lips and his. The instant his mouth touched hers, he knew he'd been right to pursue this course of action.

Dear Reader,

Being invited to participate in The Takeover continuity was a massive thrill for me. From the moment the story outline arrived in my in-box, I fell in love with William Tanner and Margaret Cole, and the task of bringing their story to you, our readers, was a willingly accepted challenge.

I've always adored a Pygmalion type of story, the whole Cinderella transformation and the knowledge that true beauty, while not always immediately visible, lies in the many layers that make up a person.

Seeing Margaret through Will's eyes was incredibly interesting. His first interaction with her was based on an instant and consuming attraction yet, as in *Cinderella,* Will had to work to track her down and find a way to make her his. Not such an easy task when he's essentially the "hit man" for Cameron Enterprises, and the livelihood of Margaret and many of her friends and colleagues relies on Will's recommendations to his boss, Rafe Cameron. Of course, seeing Will through Margaret's eyes is equally interesting as she crosses personal barriers in her own pursuit of happiness.

I hope you love this installment in The Takeover as much as I enjoyed working on it.

With very best wishes, always,

Yvonne Lindsay

YVONNE LINDSAY

BOUGHT: HIS TEMPORARY FIANCÉE

Special thanks and acknowledgment to Yvonne Lindsay for her contribution to The Takeover miniseries.

ISBN-13: 978-0-373-73091-9

BOUGHT: HIS TEMPORARY FIANCÉE

Recycling programs for this product may not exist in your area.

www.eHarlequin.com

Printed in U.S.A.

One

He was just as heart-stoppingly gorgeous as the first time she'd laid eyes on him. And those lips…

Margaret Cole stepped into William Tanner's office and couldn't tear her gaze from her new boss's mouth as he introduced himself as CFO of Cameron Enterprises— the company that had bought out Worth Industries. She'd heard he was from New Zealand originally. She wondered briefly if his home country's British colonial background was responsible for that slightly stiff-upper-lip way he had of speaking. Oh, Lord, there she was, fixated on his lips again. And no wonder. That very mouth had claimed hers in a kiss that had seared her senses and made her toes curl only six short weeks ago.

Even now she could remember the pressure of his mouth against hers, of the way her blood had suddenly heated, then rushed through her veins. The sensation more exhilarating and intoxicating than anything she'd ever experienced before.

She'd wanted more then, and she wanted more now, but men like William Tanner were pretty much off-limits for a girl like her. Especially a man who probably paid more for a single cut of his neatly trimmed dark brown hair than she spent on her own hair in a year. Not that he appeared vain. Far from it. With his casual elegance he probably never thought twice about the cost, never had to. Nor the price of the tailored business suit that fitted the width of his shoulders and now hung open, revealing his flat stomach and lean hips. Even with the two-inch heels on her sensible pumps boosting her height to five foot nine, he stood a good five inches taller than her.

Maggie found herself nodding and murmuring in response to Mr. Tanner's invitation to sit down. She really needed to gather her wits about her, but for the life of her she just couldn't. Every cell in her body vibrated on full alert. Did he recognize her from behind the elaborate mask she'd worn? She'd certainly recognized him—although, on that night, she hadn't had any idea of who he was until after the kiss that had surpassed her every fantasy.

The second he'd arrived at the company Valentine's Day ball, she'd felt his presence like a tangible thing. He'd entered the room alone, standing for a moment in the doorway, his dark costume fitted to his body, his cloak swirling gently around him. Her eyes had been instantly drawn to him. Dressed like Zorro, he was the perfect foil to her Spanish lady and it hadn't taken him long to find her and swing her away in his arms to the dance floor. They'd danced the minutes until midnight together, and he'd kissed her just as the countdown to unmasking had begun. But then someone had called his name, and as he'd taken his lips from hers she'd realized exactly who he was.

Her behavior that night had been completely out of character. She would never in a million years have believed she could feel so much so soon, for a man she'd never met before that night. A flush of heat surged through her body at the memory. A surge that came to a rapid halting crash as she became aware that he clearly awaited a response to something he'd said.

She cleared her throat nervously and fixed her gaze on a point just past his ear.

"I'm sorry, could you repeat that please?"

He smiled, no more than a smooth curve of his lips, and her internal temperature slid up another notch. This was insane. How on earth was she going to work for the man when she couldn't keep her wits about her in his presence? She'd be out of here in two seconds flat if she couldn't perform. He had a real reputation for being a hard-ass. She could deal with that. He hadn't gotten where he was at the age of thirty-one without that particular character trait, she was sure. Focused people didn't scare her—she admired them—but in his case she had to admit that she admired him just a little bit too much.

"Are you nervous?" he asked.

"No, not exactly. Perhaps a little surprised at my appointment—not that I'm complaining about it."

"I was merely commenting on your length of service with Worth Industries. You're what, twenty-eight, and you've been with Worth for eight years?"

Even his voice was a distraction. Rich and deep and with a texture that sent a tiny shiver of longing down her spine. And his accent. A little bit Upper East Side and a little bit Kiwi. The combination and inflections in his tone did crazy things to her insides.

"Yes. My whole family has worked, or does work, for Worth."

"Ah, yes, your brother—Jason, is it?"

She nodded. "And my parents, too, when they were alive. They were both on the factory floor."

"That's quite a loyal streak you're showing there."

Maggie shrugged. "Not really. Especially when you consider that Worth Industries—I mean, Cameron Enterprises—is the major industry and employer in Vista del Mar."

This promotion to Mr. Tanner's executive assistant, even in its temporary capacity, since he'd been seconded to Vista del Mar short-term only to complete financial viability studies, was not only unexpected, but the increase in income would prove very welcome. Paying off her brother's college tuition was an ongoing cost for both Jason and her, and one they looked forward to seeing the end of. Even with Jason working here for the past two years and contributing to their monthly expenses, including the payments on the small house that had been their home from childhood, the college loans had remained a yoke around their necks. Maybe now, with her promotion, they could plan for a few luxuries for themselves—within reason, of course.

"Have you never wanted to branch out? Go further afield with your work?" he asked, leaning back against the edge of his desk.

Go further afield? She was afraid if she told him the truth he'd laugh at her. Ever since she was a child she'd had a map of the world pinned to her bedroom wall—a round red pin pressed into every city or country she wanted to visit. For now, she contented herself with travel books and DVDs. But one day she'd fulfill those dreams.

William Tanner awaited an answer. *Wow, way to go on impressing the new boss,* she thought. So far she'd let her mind wander, what, how many times?

"Travel isn't my priority right now," she said firmly, and sat a little straighter in her chair.

He gave her another one of those smiles and she felt it all the way to the pit of her belly. She'd travel to the ends of the world with *him,* she thought and allowed her lips to curve into an answering smile.

"There may be some travel involved in your position with me. Will that be a problem?"

"No, not at all. I have no dependants."

While that was technically true, and she and Jason shared their family home, the habits of ten years were pretty darn hard to break. Besides, she still felt a deep sense of responsibility toward her younger brother. He'd gone through a very rocky time after their parents died. Guiding his decisions had become second nature, although she knew he sometimes resented her continued interest in his whereabouts and friends.

"I'm glad to hear it." He shoved his hands into his trouser pockets and pushed up off the desk edge, pacing over to one of the floor-to-ceiling windows that looked out over the Cameron Enterprises corporate campus. "You mentioned you were surprised to be given this position. Why is that?"

Maggie blinked several times behind her glasses. Surprised? Of course she was surprised. For eight years she'd been virtually invisible to her peers and certainly invisible when it had come to her previous applications for promotion.

"Well…" She chewed her lip for a moment, choosing her words carefully. "As you said, I've been here quite a while. I guess I thought that no one ever saw me as capable of rising to a position such as this. That's not to say that I don't think I am capable—nothing could be further from the truth. I've worked in several departments here and I believe my experience makes me a valuable asset to any of the executives."

He laughed. "You don't need to convince me, Margaret. You already have the job."

She felt a heated blush rise from her chest to her throat before flooding her cheeks with color. Now she'd be all blotchy. She forced herself to remain calm and focused instead on the fact he'd called her Margaret. No one called her that. Since she was a little girl everyone around her had called her Maggie, and she hadn't really minded much. But hearing her full name from his lips made it sound special, particularly with the way he spoke with that slightly clipped intonation. Yes, as the executive assistant to the CFO of Cameron Enterprises, she would be called Margaret. She replayed the syllables in her mind and let a small smile play across her face in response.

"Thank you, I do know that. I just want you to know you won't be sorry you chose me."

"Oh, no, I know I won't be sorry," he replied.

Will looked across his temporary office at the woman he'd specifically requested be brought to him. It was almost impossible to believe that behind those owlish, dark-framed old-fashioned glasses and the poorly fitted suit lay the siren who'd infiltrated his dreams every night since the masquerade ball. But it was definitely her. Even with her long black hair scraped off her face and dragged into a knot that was tight enough to give *him* a headache, there was no denying the delicate line of jaw and the fine straight nose were those of his Spanish lady.

His gut tightened in anticipation. He'd waited quite long enough to revisit that kiss. Tracking her down hadn't been the easiest thing he'd ever done, but he wasn't known for his tenaciousness for nothing. The trait had stood him well over the years and gave him an edge that saw him succeed where others failed. And he would succeed with the delectable Ms. Cole—he had no doubt about it.

She'd done a runner on him the night of the ball, but not before enticing him in a way no other woman had—ever. He wasn't a man to be denied, not under any circumstances—

especially not when his reaction to her had been very obviously mirrored by the object of his attention.

And here she was. He blinked. It really was hard to believe they were one and the same woman. She fidgeted in her chair—a reminder that it was up to him to do something about the silence that now stretched between them.

"Tell me about your time here. I see from your file that you spent some time in the factory before moving into office work?"

"Yes," she replied, her deceptively prim lips pursed slightly as she appeared to choose her next words carefully. "I started in the factory, but the shifts made it difficult for me to be available for my brother before and after school. I requested a transfer into admin and learned what I know now from the ground up."

"Available for your brother?"

A cloud filled her dark brown eyes and she took her time before responding.

"Yes, that's right. Our parents died when I was eighteen and for the first couple of years afterward we got by on a small insurance policy my father had left us. Of course, that wasn't going to take care of us forever and Jason was still in school so it made sense that I find work. Worth Industries was pretty much the only place that was hiring at the time."

None of this was news to him but it was good to know his sources had been accurate in their dissemination of information.

"That can't have been easy for you."

"No, it wasn't."

Again, a careful response. One that answered, but failed to give any details. Clearly his Ms. Cole was one to keep her cards close to her chest—and what a chest. Even the unbelievably unflattering cut of her suit failed to hide the lush curves of her body. For someone who appeared to actively want to hide her attributes, she still maintained deliciously perfect posture. It was that very upright bearing that confirmed his first impressions of her had been spot on. Margaret Cole was all woman, with the type of figure that would have seen her painted on the nose cowl of every fighter plane in aviation history.

Will forced his thoughts back to the business at hand.

"And I see you've been here, on the financial floor, for the past five years."

"I like numbers," she said with a small smile. "They tend to make better sense than other things."

He smiled back; he felt exactly the same way. His eldest brother, Michael, worked in human resources back in New York. To this day the problems Mike faced and relished each day made Will's head ache. He'd rather face a root canal than that. There was comfort in the cohesion of working with numbers. The defined parameters, yet with infinite possibilities were the types of challenges he excelled at. Which brought him very squarely back to the woman seated in front of him.

"Most of what you'll be doing for me will probably fall outside the usual reports and things you've been doing for middle management here."

"I enjoy a challenge," Margaret answered back.

"I'm glad to hear it. Here, let's get you started on something I've been working on." He reached across his desk and grabbed the file that lay in solitary splendor on the highly polished surface. "Take a look at that and give me your first impressions."

Margaret accepted the file from him and he saw her forehead wrinkle into a small frown as she concentrated on the report. He leaned his hip against his desk and simply watched her as her lips pursed while she read through the columns. Did she give everything in her life that intense concentration? he wondered. The prospect was both intriguing and enticing and occupied his thoughts as she thumbed methodically through the pages.

She must indeed have had a good head for figures, because she closed the folder after about ten minutes and looked him square in the eye.

"It would seem that the figures don't match up. The error margin isn't large, but it's consistent."

Her quick discernment gave him a punch of delight. Not only beautiful under that frumpy disguise, but sharply intelligent, too. The knowledge made him look forward all the more to what he'd planned.

"Good," he replied as he took the file back from her. "I think we're going to work very well together. Tell me, what would you recommend if you had discovered such an anomaly?"

"Well, I'd probably suggest a deeper audit of the books—see how long this has been going on. Then perhaps a more specific check as to who has been involved with the accounts and has access to the funds."

Will nodded. "That's exactly what we have done in this case."

"So this is an ongoing investigation?"

"It's pretty much wrapped up, with the exception of one or two things."

"That's good to hear," Margaret said. "It's too easy for people to be tempted these days. Too often a little responsibility puts a person in a position where they think they're entitled to help themselves to something that's not theirs."

"Yes, well, in this case we're certain we have the culprit lined up. He will be facing a disciplinary panel later this afternoon."

"Disciplinary panel? You won't be firing him?"

"Whether we choose to fire him or not has yet to be decided. Which kind of brings me to you, really."

"Me? In what way?"

Confusion clouded her features and for a moment Will almost felt sorry for her. He knew that what he had to say next would probably rip the rug right out from under her.

"Just how close to your brother's work habits are you?"

"Jason? What? Why?"

Understanding slowly dawned on her and all the color in her face slowly drained away. If she hadn't already been seated, Will had no doubt she'd be dropping into the nearest chair by now.

"*Jason* is the one you're investigating?"

"He is." Will leaned back against his desk again and caught her gaze with a rock-hard stare. "How much do you know about what he's been up to?"

"Nothing! No! He couldn't, *wouldn't* do such a thing. He loves his work. There's no way he's capable of doing something like this. Seriously, I…"

"So you have had nothing to do with it?"

Her features froze. "Me? No, of course not! Why would you even think such a thing?"

Will shrugged. "Stranger things have happened, and you know the saying. Blood is thicker than water."

A fact he knew all too well. It was that very fact that had him in this situation with Margaret Cole in the first place. Rather than take his time, relishing her pursuit and letting it play out to its natural conclusion, his father's latest edict forced him to speed things along somewhat. If Will didn't show some sign of settling down soon, his father would sell the family sheep station back in New Zealand rather than transfer it into Will's ownership as he was supposed to have done over a year ago when Will had turned thirty.

Each of the Tanner sons had received a massive financial

settlement on their thirtieth birthday, but Will had said that rather than money he wanted the farm. His father had agreed, but that agreement seemed to now be laden with conditions Will wasn't prepared to meet. Not in truth, anyway.

It wasn't the fact that he wanted or needed the land— goodness only knew he had little enough time to travel back to his home country these days. But the farm was such a vital part of his family heritage that he couldn't bear to see it carved up into multiple parcels of "lifestyle" farms, or worse, fall into corporate or foreign ownership. The very thought that his father could so cavalierly cast off something that had been a part of all their lives was no laughing matter. That Albert Tanner was using the farm as a bargaining chip showed how very determined he was to see his youngest son settle down.

And, above everything else, it was the knowledge that his father was deeply disappointed in him that rankled. That and the fact that both his parents and his brothers couldn't seem to understand that while love and marriage were at the forefront of their minds, it wasn't at the forefront of his. Not now, maybe not ever.

"Blood might be thicker than water but there's no way I'd ever condone such a thing. Jason can't be behind this. It's just not like him. Besides, he only holds a minor position in accounting and he wouldn't have access to be able to do this."

He had to admire her loyalty to her brother. Will's digging had discovered that Jason had a none-too-smooth history, going back to when he was just a teen. While his records had been sealed by the courts because of his age at the time, money had a convenient way of finding people with a truth to tell. Jason Cole's habit of petty theft as a teenager could easily have escalated over the years into something far more sophisticated. And yet, despite everything, Margaret still believed he wasn't involved with this current situation. Well, he hated to shatter her illusions, but the truth was there in the report. The numbers didn't lie. He pressed home his advantage.

"But you have higher clearances, don't you?"

"Not for this kind of thing and even if I did, I would never share that information with anyone. Not even my brother."

She was so puffed up with righteous indignation and outrage he was tempted to tell her he believed her. But any softness would remove the leverage he needed right now.

"I'm very glad to hear it. The fact remains, however, that your brother is most definitely involved. All our evidence points to him. However, there is a chance he may not be prosecuted over this."

"A chance? What chance?"

Will took a deep breath. This had to go right so he needed to choose his words very carefully, indeed.

"I have a proposition that will protect your brother's position here and ensure news of his activity won't get out, nor will it be permanently recorded on his file should he leave to work for another company."

He saw the hope flare in her eyes and felt a momentary pang of regret that he had to manipulate her in this way. A pang he rapidly quashed.

"What is it? What do we need to do? Seriously, we'll do anything to protect Jason's position here."

"It's not so much what the two of you can do, although he'll definitely have to clean up his act. It's more to do with what you can do."

"Me? I don't understand."

"Your appointment as my executive assistant is a two-pronged affair. On the one hand, I need someone with your acumen and your experience to be my right hand while I'm here." He paused for a moment before continuing. "On the other, I need someone—*you,* specifically—to pose as my fiancée."

"Your what?" she gasped, shooting to her feet, her shock clearly visible on her mobile features.

"You heard me."

"Your fiancée? Are you crazy? That's just ridiculous. We don't even know one another."

"Ah, but we do."

He crossed the room in a few long strides, coming to halt directly in front of her. The light scent she wore, something floral and innocent and totally at odds with the sensual creature he knew lingered under her proper exterior, wafted on the air between them. Will lifted his hand and traced one finger along the enticing fullness of her lower lip.

"Let me enlighten you."

He didn't give her so much as a split second to react. He closed the short distance between her lips and his. The instant his mouth touched hers he knew he'd been right to pursue this course of action. A powerful thrill pulled through him as her lips opened beneath the coaxing pressure of his, as her taste invaded his senses and held him in her thrall. It was all he could do not to lift his hands to her hair and free it from that appalling knot and drive his fingers through its silky length.

Reason fought for supremacy and he wrenched his lips from hers in a force of will that surprised even him.

"See? We do *know* each other, and I believe we could be quite—" he paused again for effect "—convincing together."

Margaret took a couple of steps back from him. She shook from head to toe. Desire? Fear? Perhaps a combination of both he decided, watching the play of emotions across her face.

"No." She shook her head vehemently. "No, I will not do it. It's just wrong."

"Then you leave me no choice."

"No choice? In what?"

"In ensuring that a recommendation is made that formal charges be laid against your brother."

Two

"That's blackmail!"

Her heart hammered in her chest as the finality of William Tanner's words sank in. Surely he couldn't be serious?

"I prefer to call it a basis for negotiation," he said smoothly, as if he did this sort of thing every day.

Who knew? Maybe he did. All Maggie knew was that her usually well-ordered world had suddenly been tilted off its axis. Jason had been on the straight and narrow for years. The trouble he'd gotten into as a teen now well and truly behind him. Surely he can't have been so stupid as to dip into company funds?

She went on the attack. "You're mad. You can't do this to me—to us!"

"If by 'us,' you're referring to your brother and yourself, rest assured, I can and I am. Margaret, your brother took a risk when he started playing in the big boy's league. Embezzlement is never a good look on a résumé. Sure, this is only a beginning, but who is to say he wouldn't get more daring if I hadn't picked this up in our audit?"

Maggie watched William in horror. She processed his words as quickly as she'd processed the information in the damning report on her brother's activities. Whether Jason was guilty or not, it was doubtful that he'd escape from this without some serious scars. The last judge he'd stood before in court had made it quite clear that he was being given one final opportunity to clean up his act—and he had. She didn't want to even consider what might happen if he went before the courts again.

If what William said *was* true, then it was just as well that Jason be stopped now. But, in her heart of hearts, she didn't want to believe a word of it.

"No, he wouldn't. He promised—" She cut off her words before she gave Mr. Tanner any further ammunition to use against her brother.

"Margaret, please, sit down. Clearly this news has come as a shock, and why wouldn't it? I understand you campaigned quite hard for your brother to be given the position he now occupies."

The innuendo in his voice left its mark. He'd already intimated that she could be linked to the fraudulent activity. As innocent as she knew she was, mud had a habit of sticking. She wouldn't have a position here for long if there was any suspicion she was involved, especially not with the corporate restructuring that was rumored to be in the works. Rafe Cameron's determined takeover of Worth Industries, and almost instant rebranding to Cameron Enterprises, had left everyone feeling a little precarious with respect to their jobs. It still wasn't certain what his plans were for the company, and fresh rumors arose each day about the likelihood of the factory work being outsourced to Mexico or, worse, the whole company being moved closer to Cameron's home base in New

York—which would mean the loss of almost all their jobs. Several top-level executive heads had already rolled, or been ousted on the basis of early retirement. And then there was the steady stream of Cameron's own people coming into those key roles, William Tanner being one of them. A shiver ran down her spine.

She swallowed back the words she longed to say. The words that would set William Tanner straight on exactly where she stood on matters of honesty and loyalty. Common sense held her back. Granted, it had been six years since Jason's last run-in with the law. She'd lost track of the number of times she'd been called to the local police station to collect him after he'd been picked up for one misdemeanor or another, in the first couple of years after their parents died. But then the trouble had started to get worse—so much so that Officer Garcia could no longer let Jason go with a stern lecture and a promise of dire things to come.

The first—and last—time Jason had been locked up he was eighteen. The experience of being charged as an adult, with all its long-term ramifications, had finally opened his eyes to his behavior. He'd promised her that would be the only time, and that he'd learned his lesson, big-time. He even swore on their parents' graves that he'd stay away from trouble for the rest of his life. She'd believed him—believed *in* him—so much so that she'd increased the mortgage over the home they'd grown up in so she could borrow the money necessary to send him to college out of state. Somewhere he could start afresh. Somewhere he could grow into the man she and their parents had always believed he would be.

Was it possible he'd thrown that all away?

"Look—" William butted in on her thoughts "—the way I see it, we'd be doing each other a favor."

"A favor?" she repeated dully.

What kind of favor saw her lose everything she held dear?

She'd fought long and hard to maintain her dignity through years of adversity and a lack of recognition. She had always aspired to do better—to be more. Now it appeared that everything she had ever done had been for nothing. Now she was expected to *prostitute* herself to save her brother.

"In return for you doing this for me, and believe me, you will be very well compensated, I will ensure that your brother receives nothing more than a reprimand. Obviously he'll be under close supervision. If he keeps out of trouble, this transgression will be removed from his staff record and he'll have a clean slate once more."

"And if I don't?"

"You will both be escorted from the premises immediately and I imagine that we can arrange for the police to be waiting for you at the front door. It'd probably take some time to go to trial, but I can assure you that if it did, there would be no question of Jason being found guilty."

William Tanner's voice was adamant. Each word a cold steel nail in the coffin of what had been her dreams.

"How long?" she asked.

"How long what?"

"How long would I have to pretend?"

She injected enough distaste in her voice to make William's eyes narrow as he appeared to consider his answer.

"Don't think this would be a walk in the park, Margaret. If you take this on you will have to be convincing in your role." When she didn't reply, he continued. "My father has put some pressure upon me to follow in my brothers' footsteps and find a good woman to settle down with. At this stage of my career that is the furthest thing from my mind. He's withholding something that is rightfully mine over this issue, and the situation is distressing my mother. I would need you to be my fiancée until I'm assured that the transfer of ownership of property back in New Zealand takes place. Basically, until my family calms down again and continues to act reasonably."

"So there's no finite term on this?"

Margaret could feel the walls closing in on her now. With his open-ended proposal and the continued threat of Jason losing his job hanging overhead, this would be a total nightmare. One from which she was afraid she might never awake. And yet this morning had started so promisingly with the inter-office communication confirming that she'd been promoted to being Tanner's EA. For Margaret, the only way from a position like this was up and her summons to report to his office this afternoon had been something she'd been looking forward to all day.

"Obviously this won't go on forever. It's not as if we'll be getting married."

He said the words as if the entire prospect of marriage was completely abhorrent to him.

"Let me get this clear. You want me to pretend to be your fiancée for an undetermined period of time. In exchange you'll recompense me and you will ensure that Jason doesn't lose his job."

"That Jason doesn't lose his job over *this* incident. Should he push his boundaries and try something a little more sophisticated there will be no more second chances."

No more second chances. The words were exactly what the judge had said when Jason had been brought before the court. She'd never been certain if it was the judge's words or the night he'd spent in the county jail's holding cells that had been the catalyst he'd needed to finally want to break free from the creeps he'd been hanging out with. She hadn't cared much at the time. All she'd been concerned with was getting her brother back on an even keel. It had cost her far more than money to do so and she wasn't about to jeopardize things now.

Margaret knew she wasn't in a position to argue, but never in her wildest dreams had she imagined she would be forced into something like this. It wasn't enough that the man had infiltrated her private thoughts and fantasies in the six weeks since the Valentine's Day ball. Now he would control her days as well.

"Why? Why me?" she whispered.

He reached out a finger to trace her lips.

"Because you intrigue me, Margaret Cole. You intrigue me very much."

Despite her distress, she reacted to his caress as if it was a touch of lightning. Her lips parted on a sharply indrawn breath and deep to her core she felt the sizzling awareness of his touch.

"Margaret," he continued, "if you truly believe your brother to be innocent in this, you owe it to him to allow him to prove it. He can't do that if he's suspended pending further investigation, can he?"

Blood pounded in her ears, almost drowning out his words. Her chest tightened with anxiety. What choice did she have? In her heart she knew that Jason could not have done what he was being accused of, but the evidence said differently. She did owe him the chance to prove his innocence. If she didn't accede to Mr. Tanner's demands, all the hard years of work she'd put into Jason, and all the effort he'd made to clean up his act and make something of himself would be in vain.

She drew in a shaky breath.

"I'll do it," she said, the words little more than a whisper. She stood up and raised her head to meet William Tanner square in the eye. "I'll do it," she repeated, more strongly this time.

Will could barely hold back the rush of excitement that spread with molten heat through his body. She'd agreed. For a few moments there he'd thought she'd refuse—that maybe she'd throw her brother to the wolves and to hell with the consequences. He should have trusted his initial research. Margaret Cole was intensely loyal. Everyone had spoken highly of her, from the factory floor workers who still remembered her parents all the way through to the middle management for whom she'd provided secretarial support. As hard as he'd tried, he hadn't been able to unearth the smallest speck of dirt on his elusive masked Spanish lady—except for what her brother had handed him on a platter.

And now, she was his. All his.

"I'm glad to hear it," he said with a quick smile. "I believe it would be best if you went home now. I'll talk to you in the morning about your instructions."

"Instructions?" A spark of fire burned in her eyes.

"As to your new duties, of course. You haven't held an EA role before so I don't expect you to fall immediately into place. And then, of course, there are your extracurricular duties to discuss as well."

A tremor ran through her body. Was it revulsion? He doubted it. Not after the way she'd reacted to him during that all too brief kiss a few minutes ago and especially not after he'd seen the fire leap to life in her eyes as he'd traced the soft fullness of her lower lip with only a fingertip. With her response being so instinctive, so honest, he knew the next few weeks, even months, would undoubtedly be as pleasurable as he'd anticipated from the moment he'd laid eyes on her.

He took a step toward her and tried to tamp down the disappointment he felt when he saw her flinch. Sure, he knew she'd be reluctant. What woman wouldn't under these circumstances? But he had her exactly where he needed her and she couldn't run away.

"I don't need to remind you that this matter between us is completely confidential. Of course there will be questions when news of our 'engagement' leaks out, but I'm hoping we can keep them under control if we keep our stories straight."

"Jason and I share our home. I have to tell him, at least."

"I'd prefer you didn't. Obviously I can't stop you two from discussing the accusations against him, but the more people who know our engagement is a sham the more likely it is to be exposed."

"Don't you understand? Jason and I live together. I can't hide the truth from him."

"Then you'll have to convince him that you're doing this for love."

"Believe me, he won't have any trouble with that. He knows I love him."

"No. Not him. *Me*."

To his surprise, a throaty laugh bubbled from her. As delectable as the sound was, the reason behind it wasn't. He bristled, going on the defensive.

"Is that so very hard to believe?" he pressed. "Don't you think you'll be able to act with credibility?"

"No, please, you misunderstand me." She sobered instantly, the moment of hysteria passed even though traces of moisture still lingered in the corners of her eyes. "You don't know me or you wouldn't ever have suggested we could fake our engagement. I don't go out, I…"

Her hesitation hung in the air between them.

"Yes, you…?"

She threw her hands up, gesturing to herself. "Well, look at me. I'm hardly the kind of woman you'd go out with under normal circumstances, am I? I don't move in your circles, I'm…I'm me." She shrugged her shoulders dramatically, as if that was sufficient explanation for everything.

"Do you want to see who I see when I look at you, Margaret?"

He kept his voice steady and pitched low. Her nervous

movements stilled at his tone and he saw her brace herself, physically and mentally, for whatever it was that he had to say.

"I see a woman who hides her true self from the world. Someone who has a deep inner beauty to match the exterior. Someone who would go so far as to sacrifice her own happiness for that of a loved one. I see a woman who doesn't realize the extent of her own potential, at work or in play. And I see a woman I am very much looking forward to getting to know, intimately."

The flush that spread up her throat and across her cheeks was as intriguing as it was enticing. Was she really so innocent that she blushed at his suggestion? She hadn't thought this fake engagement was going to be purely for appearances, did she? There had to be fringe benefits—for them both.

"So you're going to force me to have sex with you, too, are you?" she asked, her voice wavering slightly.

"Oh, no," William replied. "I won't have to force you at all."

Margaret was still shaking when she made it to her car in the back row of the staff car park. She shoved her key in the door and gave it the customary wiggle she needed to do before turning it and opening the door. She clambered inside and put her key in the ignition. Since her car had been stolen a year ago, both the door lock and the new ignition barrel hadn't been quite in sync with the key. She'd been lucky that when the car was recovered a few miles from home that it was still drivable. One of Jason's friends, an auto mechanic, had done the minor repair work for her at cost. It hadn't been the same since then, though. One day it would let her down, but hopefully not any day too soon.

She rested her head on the steering wheel. It wasn't the only thing that wasn't the same anymore. How could she look at Jason now without worrying about whether he was getting himself into trouble again? No matter what William Tanner had dictated, she would tell Jason the truth about their arrangement. Provided he agreed to be sworn to secrecy, that is.

Maggie wasn't looking forward to what kind of state he'd be in when he got home after the disciplinary panel today, but she knew he wouldn't be happy with her "engagement." With a sigh, she straightened in her seat, started up the car and headed for home. She might find some answers there, or at least some solace in being surrounded by their parents' things.

Grief lanced through her with a sharp, searing pain. Ten years since the accident that had taken both their lives and it still hurt as much as it had when the police had come to the door to give them the news. Where would they be now, she wondered, if her parents hadn't died that day?

She shook her head. There was no point in dwelling on the past. The present, that was what mattered. Making every day count. Meeting the obligations she'd shouldered when she'd made the decision to forgo college and focus on raising Jason alone. At eighteen to his fourteen it had been a monumental decision—one she'd frequently questioned as she'd faced each new trial. But the Cole family had never been quitters. They stuck to their own, through thick and thin. No matter the cost.

By the time Jason arrived home, an hour later than usual, her nerves were tied in knots. The sound of his key being shoved in the front door, followed by the heavy slam as it closed, did not augur well for a rational discussion.

"Are you okay?" she asked as he came through to the kitchen where she was reheating last night's Bolognese sauce and meatballs.

"It's un-freaking-believable," he said. "I've been accused

of stealing, but not quite enough that they're going to take my job from me. I'm on some kind of big-brother probation."

"I know," she said, struggling to keep her voice calm.

"You know? And you didn't think to tell me? Give me any prior warning?"

His voice was filled with confusion and accusation. Inside, her heart began to break.

"I couldn't. I was only told of it right before your meeting with the disciplinary panel."

Jason dragged his cell phone from his pocket and waved it in her face. "Hello? You could have texted me."

"I didn't have a chance. Seriously, you have to believe me. I would have, if I could."

He dropped into one of the bentwood kitchen chairs, the old wooden frame creaking in protest as he threw his weight against the back of the seat and shoved a hand through his dark hair. Unbidden, tears sprang to Maggie's eyes. Times like this he reminded her so much of photos of their father when he was younger. All that intelligence, energy and passion. All so easily misdirected.

She dropped down on her haunches beside him.

"Tell me. What did they say?"

He looked up at the ceiling and swore softly under his breath. "You know what they said. They're accusing me of taking money, but they don't have absolute proof it was me. Anyone could have made that trail go in someone else's direction. I've been framed. I wouldn't do something like that."

Her stomach knotted at the almost childlike plea in his voice. A plea that she, above all others, would believe him.

"Did you, Jason? Did you do it?"

He thrust himself up onto his feet. "I can't believe you can even ask me that. I promised you I'd be clean after that last time and I have been."

"Mr. Tanner showed me the evidence, Jason. He said everything pointed to you."

She felt as if she was drowning. She wanted to believe Jason, really she did. But William Tanner had been very convincing. So convincing she'd agreed to participate in his charade to save Jason's job.

"So you'd rather believe him than me? Is that it? Are you still so goo-goo eyed after that one kiss at the ball that you don't want to believe your own brother?"

"Jason, that's uncalled for," she replied sharply, but she felt the betraying flush stain her cheeks.

Her brother had teased her mercilessly about the kiss he'd witnessed at the ball, until he'd learned exactly who it was she'd been kissing. William Tanner was a man to be feared. No one knew exactly what his recommendation would be for the now defunct Worth Industries, and the rumors that the business could be wound down here in Vista del Mar had buzzed around the staff like a swarm of angry bees.

"I don't believe it," he said, staring at her as if she'd grown two heads. "Even though he's accused me of being dishonest, you still have the hots for him, don't you?"

"This isn't about me." She tried desperately to get the conversation back on topic. "This is about you. I asked you, plain and simple, Jason. Did you do it?"

"It doesn't matter what I say now," he said bleakly. "You're never going to believe me, are you? I'll never be good enough, never be able to prove to you that I'm trustworthy again. Don't wait up for me, I'm going out."

"Jason, don't go. Please!"

But his only response was the slam of the front door behind him, swiftly followed by the roar of his motorbike as he peeled out of the driveway. Margaret raised a trembling hand to her eyes and wiped at the tears that fell unchecked down her cheeks.

If Jason was guilty of what Tanner had accused him, then she would continue to do every last thing in her power to protect him, just as she always had. But if he was innocent, what on earth had she let herself in for?

Three

Maggie was beyond worried by the time morning came. Jason hadn't been home all night. Around four she'd given up trying to sleep and had done what she always did in times of stress—clean. By the time seven-thirty rolled around, the bathroom sparkled, the kitchen bench gleamed and every wooden surface in the house shone with the glow of the special lemon-scented polish their mother had always used.

The scents were in their own way a little comfort, Maggie thought, as she finally peeled off her gloves and wearily went into the kitchen to put on a pot of coffee. She could almost feel her mother's soothing presence in the background.

The growl of Jason's bike as he pulled into the driveway had her flying to the door. She yanked it open, then froze in the doorway. Uncertain of whether or not he would welcome her relief at seeing him home safe and sound.

He came to the door slowly, his face haggard and showing a wisdom beyond his years.

"I'm sorry, Maggie," he said, pulling her into his arms and hugging her tight. "I was so mad I just had to put some space between me and here, y'know?"

She nodded, unable to speak past the knot in her throat. He was home. That was all that mattered for now. She led him inside, pushed him into one of the kitchen chairs and set about making breakfast. As she broke eggs into the pan he started to talk.

"At least I still have my job."

"Yes, you do," Maggie replied. He still didn't know her news, she realized. He wouldn't be happy when he knew. She took a steadying breath. "Speaking of work…"

"What?" Jason asked sharply, picking up on her unease instantly.

"I got a promotion yesterday." May as well transition into this slowly, she thought.

"You did? That's great." Although Jason said the words, the lack of enthusiasm in his voice spoke volumes. "Ironic, huh? The day I get a final written warning and supervision, you get bumped up the ladder. So what are you doing?"

"I've been offered an executive assistant position. It's only temporary for now, but I'm hoping it'll lead to better things in the future." Much, much better things.

"That's cool, Maggie. Who to?"

She stiffened her spine. He wasn't going to like this one bit.

"William Tanner."

"You're kidding me. That insufferable jerk? He was the one who headed the panel yesterday. You didn't take it, did you?" Realization dawned slowly. "You did. That's how you knew about what happened to me."

"I had to, Jason. He didn't leave me any option."

"What? He forced you to take a promotion? You should

have told him to stick it where the sun don't shine." He made a sound of disgust and shook his head.

"Jason, he was going to go to the police over you."

"But I told you I didn't do it."

"All the evidence points to you, Jase. Unless you can prove otherwise, he holds all the strings, including mine." Maggie sighed and reached out to ruffle his hair. "It's not so bad, really. I get a raise in salary."

She balked at telling him the rest of Mr. Tanner's demands. He'd totally flip if he knew.

"I still don't like it. I don't trust the guy," Jason grumbled as he gently swatted her hand away. "You had better not have agreed to work for him to keep my job safe."

She couldn't answer him. She heard his sound of exasperation.

"You did, didn't you? How, in all that's logical, did you agree to that?"

"There's more to it," Margaret started, only to be cut off by her brother.

"Oh, yeah, sure there is. With men like him there always is. So what is it? Is he looking to pick up where you two left off back in February? Is that what it is?"

"Something like that. You can't tell anyone, Jason. Promise me you won't say a word of this to anyone."

"Yeah, like I'm going to shout to the rooftops that my sister is sleeping with her boss to save my job?"

"I'm not sleeping with him! Might I remind you that I have *you* to thank for putting me in this position in the first place? He's asked me to stand in as his fiancée, only for a short time while he sorts something out."

"His what?"

Maggie was saved from further explanation by the interruption of their phone. She lifted the receiver and cradled it between her ear and shoulder as she dished up Jason's scrambled eggs.

"Margaret, it's William Tanner."

She'd have recognized his voice anywhere. The tiny hairs on her arms and up the back of her neck prickled with awareness, her whole body tautening in response.

"Good morning," she replied as coolly as she could. She reached across the table and put Jason's plate in front of him before retreating to the living room.

"Look, I know it's early, but I wanted to catch you before you went into the office and wasted yourself a trip."

"Wasted a trip?"

Didn't he want her anymore? While a part of her sagged with relief, another leaped into full alert. Did this mean that they were going to fire Jason anyway?

"I need you to meet me here at the Vista Del Mar Beach and Tennis Club. I'll let them know at reception that I'm expecting you. How soon can you be here?"

Maggie knew that Rafe Cameron's team of executives involved in the takeover were being put up in the guest accommodations at the club. Her friend, Sarah Richards, worked there in the main restaurant and had commented on the influx of long-stay guests. Maggie took a quick glance at the mantel clock her father had been given for thirty years' service at Worth Industries. If she was quick getting ready, she could make it by eight-thirty, traffic permitting.

"By half past eight," she said into the phone, mentally cataloging her wardrobe to decide on what to wear today.

"See if you can't make it sooner."

Before she could respond, she realized she was listening to the disconnect signal on the phone. "Right, sure thing, boss, anything you say," she said as she hit the "off" button and took the phone back through to the kitchen.

"Problem?" Jason asked through a mouthful of egg.

"No. I just need to meet Mr. Tanner at the club this morning."

"Maybe he wants to check out your forehand before you start working for him," he commented snidely.

Maggie remained silent. She had no idea what he really wanted her for. It could be anything. Yet, strangely, the thought didn't strike fear into her heart. Instead, there was a fine shimmer of anticipation. She clamped down on the feeling before it could take wings. Whatever she was to meet him for was not optional—she needed to remind herself of that. He had her between a rock and a hard place. What she wanted, what she *really* wanted, had no significance beyond keeping Jason out of prison.

Will straightened his tie before checking his Rolex. She was late. Not exactly the most auspicious start for their first day of work together. He crossed the sitting room of the self-contained beachfront suite that was his temporary home and waited out on the terrace overlooking the Pacific. Waves rolled in with steady force, pounding the sand of the perfectly groomed beach before sucking back and starting all over again. He smiled. Even here, he was reminded of his family. Relentless. Well, they'd have to take a step back when they found out about Margaret, that was for sure. Although it wouldn't do for them to discover her too soon. If he was to suddenly produce a fiancée within a month of his last argument with his father it would only look suspicious.

A timid knock at the door barely caught his attention. Ah, she was finally here. He opened the door wide to admit her.

"Traffic bad?" he asked as she entered on his bidding.

"I'm sorry I'm late. Yes, some contractors hit a water main on my street just after you called. It was chaos getting out of there."

She looked flustered, although for someone who'd probably

missed her morning shower because of the issue with the
water main she still managed to come across in her usual
competent manner. Competent being the kindest way to
describe the shapeless beige suit she wore today. He fought
back a grimace.

"Is there something wrong?" she asked.

"No, nothing that can't be rectified today, at least," he
responded.

Why did she dress in such awful clothing? he wondered.
He'd caught a glimpse of her hourglass figure in the gown
she'd worn at the ball, felt the lush fullness of her curves when
he'd kissed her. Even now his hands itched to push away the
serviceable fabric of her jacket and shape themselves to her
form.

"What would you like me to do today?" she asked.

She stood perfectly straight and tall in her sensible pumps,
awaiting his instruction. Will toyed with the idea of what
would happen if he asked her to disrobe and burn the clothes
she wore right now, but discarded it for the foolishness it
was.

"As my executive assistant, and as my fiancée, there will
be certain expectations."

She blanched at his words. "Expectations. Right. Perhaps
we'd better discuss those now."

"Trying to call the shots, Margaret? That's a little late,
don't you think?" he teased.

"I think you should know, there are some things I absolutely
won't do," she answered with a defiant tilt of her chin.

"I'm sure there are," he responded smoothly, deciding to
err on the side of caution for now. "But I hope those things
don't include shopping."

"Shopping? For you?"

"No. For you. I'm sure what you're wearing was perfectly
serviceable for your previous position but I expect a little more

from my immediate staff. Besides, as my fiancée, people will certainly have something to say if you continue to dress in—" he gestured at her from shoulder to feet "—that."

She stiffened at his words. "I have a very careful budget, Mr. Tanner. And I try to buy clothes that won't date."

Won't date, he thought. How about won't get past first base altogether.

"I don't expect you to pay for these new items, Margaret. Consider them a fringe benefit. I have an image consultant coming to meet us shortly. Paige Adams—you may have heard of her. I understand she comes highly recommended. She'll take us out this morning to start getting you prepared for your new role."

"I'm going to spend the whole day shopping?" she asked, her eyes wide with surprise.

"Probably not the whole day, no. I'm sure Ms. Adams will have some other things up her sleeve to make your transformation complete."

"And will you be accompanying us on this...this expedition?"

She made it sound like an unwelcome hunting trip.

"Until about two. I have meetings this afternoon that I can't get out of so I'll have to leave you in her hands at that stage but I will see you for dinner tonight."

"Do I get any choice in this?"

There was that delicious hint of steel in her voice, as if beneath the timidity she really did have a will of iron. For some reason, Will found that incredibly appealing. Would she be like that in the bedroom? he wondered. Would she be sweet and compliant, then take control? Take him? An unexpected flood of heat suffused him, sending blood to his groin in a torrent of need.

"Oh, yes. You will have a choice." He hesitated and saw the way her shoulders relaxed, how her chest filled with air, the way her generous breasts moved beneath the serviceable fabric of her suit jacket, before continuing, "Up to a point."

"I won't let you dress me to look like some whore."

Ah, there it was again. That edge of strength. Will forced himself to rein in the urge to cross the distance between them and show her just how good it would be to let him take charge. Too soon, he reminded himself.

"Don't worry, that's the furthest thing from my mind," he said.

A knock at the door interrupted the weighted silence that spread between them.

"That'll be Ms. Adams."

He crossed the carpeted sitting room of his suite and swung open the heavy wooden door.

Margaret stood exactly where he'd left her. Focusing on each inward and outward breath. This was going to be so much more difficult than she'd anticipated. Yesterday it had sounded so simple. Work as his executive assistant. Pretend to be his fiancée. *Keep Jason out of jail.*

But the thought of William Tanner selecting her clothing, of him grooming her so specifically for the role she'd agreed to take on, sent a shiver of caution rippling through her. How would she stand it? She, who so carefully chose her work attire from Time Again, a thrift store supplied by the more affluent areas in town. Everything she bought was good quality, if a little dated. Did it really matter that much?

Imagining him waiting outside the dressing room as she tried on items of clothing for *his* approval made her uncomfortable just thinking about it. Uncomfortable, and something else. Something that went deeper than the idea that a man would have the final say on what she wore and how she looked on a daily basis. Something that sent a throb of longing from a place deep inside of her—a place she'd ruthlessly controlled and held in submission from the day she'd assumed guardianship of Jason.

She had responsibilities. Sure she'd had the occasional boyfriend, some had even become lovers—she was, after all, only human. But she'd never allowed herself to take a step beyond that—to allow herself to fully engage her feelings. Right now, she had the distinct impression it was going to be a whole lot more difficult to keep that distance from William Tanner.

"Meet Paige Adams."

William's voice interrupted her thoughts and Margaret forced her concentration back to the moment. She'd been fully prepared to dislike the woman on sight, in a petty attempt to assert herself over Will's directives, but it was difficult to summon a shred of antipathy toward the vibrant young woman now standing before her. Her skin was fresh and smooth and a friendly smile wreathed her face, while her unusual violet-colored eyes shone with delight.

Dressed in a sharply tailored suit that shrieked the kind of designer chic Maggie had always wished she could pull off, and a pair of high-heeled pumps that wouldn't go astray on a show like *Sex and the City,* the woman exuded both confidence and an air of affluence with effortless ease. Her well-styled hair, tamed into a neat chignon, was a shimmering pale blond that complemented the milky tone of her smooth skin. From the look of her she probably never had to worry about how she'd looked a single day in her life.

"Ms. Adams, I'm Margaret Cole," Maggie said, deciding to take the upper hand and not allow herself to be presented as a victim to the slaughter.

"Margaret, please, call me Paige. I'm delighted to meet you. Would you excuse me?" she asked and reached for the buttons on Maggie's jacket. "I like to see what I'm working with right from the start."

Maggie stiffened as Paige's fingers nimbly flew over the solid metal buttons fastening the front of her jacket. She wore only a thin blouse beneath the confining garment. A blouse she'd only chosen because she never—absolutely never—took her jacket off in the office. An early developer, she'd learned at a very young age how best to hide what made her a magnet for undesirable attention from males of all ages. Starting with her sixth-grade classmates when she'd changed from a gangly stick insect to a curvaceous boy-magnet in the space of a few months.

Maggie's eyes flew to Will's face as Paige handed him the jacket with a distracted, "Hold this." Would he be the same as so many others? Would he forget she was actually a person and not simply a body?

His sherry brown eyes met hers as Paige appraised her project with a critical eye. Maggie waited for the moment when his eyes would drop, as every man's did, to her breasts. But he never wavered, not even for a moment, and when Paige took Maggie's jacket from him and helped her back into it, Maggie felt a bone-deep relief. Maybe being around him wasn't going to be so difficult after all.

"This is going to be wonderful," Paige said enthusiastically. "How long did you say we have?"

"We have a dinner reservation for seven-thirty this evening," Will said in response.

"Oh, that's less time than I thought. Never mind, I can do this." She reached out and gave Margaret's hand an encouraging squeeze. "*We* can do this. You're great material to work with. You won't know yourself when I'm done. Trust me."

Strangely enough, Maggie did. Despite Paige's air of command and immaculate appearance, there was a warmth about her that drew Maggie in immediately.

Paige turned to William and said, "Shall we go then?"

"Certainly." Will bowed his head slightly, a bemused smile curving his lips and revealing the slightest dimple in his right cheek. "I'm at your disposal for the next few hours, then I have to head back for some meetings and leave you two to it."

Maggie felt a frisson of disquiet that he'd be accompanying them. It wasn't something he hadn't already told her, and since he was paying for everything it made sense he'd want a say in what his money went toward, but the prospect of parading before him made her incredibly nervous. She, who never tried to draw attention to herself, would now be the very center of attention. Attention from a man who she found almost irresistibly attractive.

Her pulse picked up a notch as he placed a warm hand at the small of her back and shepherded her before him as they left his suite. The action strangely intimate, and totally unsettling at the same time.

If she felt this disconcerted by something as simple as a touch, the next few hours were going to be excruciating.

Four

Excruciating didn't even begin to cover it, Maggie realized as she ducked back into the dressing room for the umpteenth time. It was as if she didn't even exist in a personal sense. She tugged off the midnight blue cocktail dress Mr. Tanner and Paige had both agreed wasn't her most flattering choice of the day and reached for a black sleeveless gown, pulling it over her head with a huff of frustration. Between the two of them she felt as if she were little more than a mannequin, right up until she shoved her feet in the matching high-heeled, black pumps that Paige had insisted she try on with the dress, and stepped outside the dressing room.

Her two torturers were sitting on the velvet-covered loveseat in the foyer of the dressing rooms, their heads together—each a perfect foil for the other—until they became aware she was standing waiting for their comment.

"Oh," said Paige, for once seemingly at a complete loss for words.

Maggie looked at William's face and her breath held fast in her lungs at the expression she saw there. The skin across his cheekbones tautened and his eyes widened and glowed in obvious appreciation.

"That's a definite," he said in a voice that sounded as if he struggled to force the words from his throat.

"Yes, it certainly is," Paige agreed.

Will rose from the seat and walked across the thick carpet to where Maggie stood nervously.

"Here, why don't we try this, just to soften things a little?"

He reached up to remove her dark-framed glasses from the bridge of her nose then folded them and tucked them in his breast pocket. He reached for Maggie's hair and pulled the pins from her habitual tight knot. Maggie felt her scalp rejoice as he tousled her hair loose from its constriction.

"Oh, yes, that's much better."

There was a note to his words that forced her to look at him, to allow her eyes to connect with his and see, without a doubt, what he was thinking. Desire flamed like a living, breathing thing and her skin tightened in response. Her breasts felt full and heavy and ached for his touch. Maggie swallowed against the sudden dryness in her throat. She was imagining things, surely. He'd said "fake" fiancée, hadn't he? But right now the expression on his face was anything but fake. His need for her was there in all honesty. A jolt of sheer lust shot through to her core, taking her breath completely away.

"Will you wear this for me tonight?" he asked.

"If you want me to," she replied, the words stilted, near impossible to force through her lips as she acknowledged the depth of feeling he aroused in her.

"You look beautiful. Nothing would give me more pleasure than to escort you looking like this. I'll be the envy of every man in the restaurant."

He smiled then, and Maggie felt her lips curve in response.

It was not so much a smile of pleasure as it was of satisfaction. For once she really felt beautiful. The admiration so clear on Will's face was a salve to her feminine soul. While she wasn't quite ready to examine how that admiration affected her on a basic level, she had to answer to the sensualist who dwelled deep within her. To deny that was nigh on impossible.

The sound of someone clearing their throat dragged Maggie's attention back to her surroundings.

"Okay, well we have a few more places to go before we're done. We've barely scratched the surface, really."

"I'll get changed," Maggie said and turned back into the dressing room.

"Here, you'd better take these," Will said, removing her spectacles from his pocket and handing them back to her.

Maggie shoved them back on her face and closed the door behind her. Faced with her own reflection in the private cubicle, she caught her breath. With her hair a loose tumble around her ivory shoulders and with the low scoop of the gown exposing the swell of her breasts she could see why Will had reacted the way he had. She scoured her memory. He hadn't dwelled on any one part of her, though. She hadn't, not even for a split second, felt uncomfortable under his perusal. She turned slowly and eyed her reflection in the mirror.

The dress was cut to perfection. If it had been made for her it couldn't have fit any better. The way it curved into her narrow waist and flared at her hips before finishing just above her knees made the most of her every attribute in a way she'd never dreamed. She skimmed her hand over the fabric before reaching for the invisible zipper sewn into the side seam. Her fingertips tingled as they slid over the fine weave. She'd never dreamed of having anything that made her feel as beautiful as this dress did. And there was still more to come.

Well, not if she didn't snap out of her reveries and get to

it, she reminded herself tersely. Even so, as she shimmied out of the dress she couldn't help but run her hands over it one more time before taking it out for Paige to add to the others William had already approved.

When she was going to wear all these garments absolutely boggled her mind—so far not one of them was suitable for the office. Aside from her regular coffee dates with her friend Gillian and the occasional catch-ups with Sarah when she wasn't working, she had little social life to speak of. All that was obviously about to change dramatically.

When she came out of the dressing room Paige was standing alone.

"Mr. Tanner had to leave early," she said, "so it's up to just us girls now."

For a split second Maggie was swamped with a sense of relief that she wouldn't have to face his minute examination of every garment and pair of shoes she tried on. But the relief was instantly tempered by the realization that it was his very approval she looked forward to every time she stepped from behind the dressing room door.

God, she was pathetic. The man was virtually blackmailing her to act as his fiancée and here she was *missing* him? How swiftly she'd fallen under his spell. Maggie needed to get her act together, and fast.

She summoned a smile and answered Paige, "That'll be fun. What's next on the agenda?"

"First we'll get these boxed up, except tonight's outfit, of course, and then I'd suggest lingerie and lunch. I'm starving, aren't you?"

Paige laughed as Maggie's stomach rumbled its own gentle response.

Later, at lunch, Paige mapped out the rest of their afternoon.

"I think we've got you covered for most social eventualities but I'd like to see you in some more feminine work wear. As soon as we're done here we'll power shop our way through some suits and then I have managed to squeeze in an appointment for you with an optometrist."

"But I can see perfectly well with these glasses," Maggie protested.

"Yes, I'm sure you can. But seriously, wouldn't you rather wear contacts? Then we can get you some super sexy sunglasses as well."

"Contacts?" Maggie wrinkled her brow. "Don't they irritate, though?"

"Not the ones these days. Let's see what they suggest, hmm? And if you're uncomfortable with contacts maybe we'll just choose some different frames for you. Something a bit softer that makes the most of your bone structure."

Maggie sat back in her chair. She'd always been too scared to try contacts before but she had to admit she was very much over the frames she'd been wearing for the past few years. One day, once all Jason's student loans were squared away, she'd maybe consider Lasik eye surgery, but that was still some time away.

"Okay, I'll give them a try," she said, making up her mind.

When Paige Adams talked makeover, she really meant *makeover,* Maggie thought later as she studied her reflection. Not only was she now wearing contact lenses, which didn't irritate her eyes, but, at the day spa at the Tennis Club, she'd been treated to a body wrap and facial, along with a pedicure and manicure. Right now, she felt both boneless and pampered. The crowning glory had come when she'd been shown to another section of the beauty spa where her hair had been subjected to a deep conditioning treatment and a restyle which saw the ends of her hair brush softly to her collarbone in soft, dark and lustrous tresses.

She barely recognized herself. The makeup artist who'd taken some time to show her how to make the most of her cheekbones and eyes had exclaimed loudly and often over how exquisite her skin was. By the time her cape was removed and the new polished and pampered Margaret Cole was revealed, even Paige let loose a long, low whistle of appreciation.

"Oh, yes," Paige said with a knowing smile. "Mr. Tanner is going to be very pleased indeed."

She cast a glance at her watch.

"We'd better get you dressed and up to his suite. It's almost seven-thirty and he doesn't strike me as the type of guy who likes to be kept waiting."

Butterflies suddenly massed in an attack squadron in the pit of her stomach. No, Will Tanner most definitely wasn't the type of guy who liked to be kept waiting.

Paige picked up the garment bag that held the black cocktail dress William had so admired, as well as the tissue-wrapped selection from the lingerie store that Paige had insisted she wear beneath it.

"Here, slip into these and let's see how gorgeous you look."

Maggie felt as if she were trapped in an alternate universe. These kinds of things just didn't happen in her world. The shopping, the makeover, the sheer quality of the stockings she slid up over her waxed and polished legs—it was like something from a dream. By the time she slid the dress carefully over her hair and makeup, and tugged the zipper closed, she was feeling a little light-headed.

She laid a hand against her stomach in a bid to quell her nerves but they simply wouldn't be suppressed.

"Everything okay in there?" Paige asked from outside the cubicle.

"Y-yes, I'm fine."

"So come on out and show us the final result," Paige coaxed.

Maggie took a deep breath, pushed her feet into the high-heeled, black pumps and took a quick look in the mirror. It wasn't her. It couldn't be. She gave herself a tentative, somewhat secretive, smile in the mirror. Even the lush ruby red painted lips didn't seem like her own.

The glamorous creature staring back at her was not the same Maggie Cole who'd left home this morning already feeling as if she was at the end of her tether. No, this was the kind of woman she'd always wished she could be but had never had the courage to reach for. This was *Margaret* Cole.

Strangely, the nerves jumping about in her belly settled and a sense of calm descended over her. She could do this. She could be the woman William Tanner needed her to be. She'd do it for Jason and, even more importantly, for herself.

Margaret closed her eyes and turned from the mirror, mentally leaving her old self behind. From now on she was Margaret Cole, fiancée and executive assistant to one of the most powerful men in Cameron Enterprises.

Both the staff of the day spa and Paige were full of praise for the final effect and it was with a sense of deep accomplishment that Margaret blushingly accepted everyone's compliments. In her hand she clutched a vintage beaded evening bag, a gift from Paige whose violet eyes had swum with tears of pride as she'd given it to her.

"Here, a little something from me," she'd said, giving Margaret a careful hug. "Now don't go all mushy on me or you'll ruin your makeup."

Margaret took the admonishment and with everyone's cheers of good wishes ringing in her ears, she approached the accommodation wing.

* * *

Will inhaled the aroma of the New Zealand Pinot Noir he'd had shipped from his cellar in New York to Vista Del Mar and anticipated savoring the myriad complex flavors that promised to dance across his taste buds. He was struck by the similarities between the simply labeled, yet award-winning wine, and the woman who was about to join him.

Today he'd caught glimpses of the siren she promised to be. The siren he hoped to have warming his sheets before too long. The siren who'd appease his father and ensure the land that had been in his family for two centuries would remain that way. He wanted the farm with a need that went soul deep. A need that had nestled in his heart from the first school holiday he'd spent tagging along behind his grandfather as he'd labored day in, day out, on the soil he loved above all other things. Even now he could still feel the strength of his grandfather's gnarled, work-worn hand holding his as they'd strolled across the fields. It had never been about the money for the old man. He'd always said there was an energy about the land that gave back to him four-fold what he put into it. And even on those rare school holiday visits, Will had understood what his grandfather had been talking about. It was a type of magic he didn't want to lose. Ever.

And now he didn't have to lose it. Margaret would undoubtedly ensure that his dream became a reality. The cost of today's exercise, already emailed to him by the ever-efficient Paige Adams, was a small investment as far as Will was concerned. One he'd make sure paid off in full.

A knock at the door made everything inside him tighten in anticipation. Slowly, deliberately, he placed the crystal wine goblet on the coffee table and went to open the door. He didn't even stop to check the peep hole. He knew to the soles of his feet exactly who stood on the opposite side.

A twist of his wrist and the door swung open to reveal

Margaret in all her glory. And what glory. For the first time in his living memory, William Tanner was speechless. His eyes feasted on the virtual stranger framed in the doorway. Every feminine curve displayed to absolute perfection. Her hair a shining swath of black silk that made his fingers itch to run through it. Her makeup so perfect that with her ivory skin she almost looked like a grown-up china doll.

Every cell in his body rejoiced. She was flawless elegance and beauty personified. Finally, he found his voice.

"You look amazing," he said, reaching for her free hand and drawing her inside to twirl her around slowly. "How do you feel?"

"Like Cinderella," Margaret admitted, with that small smile playing around her lips.

The type of smile that alluded to so much more going through her mind than the few simple words she'd spoken.

"I'm beginning to regret making the booking for dinner at Jacques' tonight," Will said.

"Oh? Why is that?"

"Because I don't know if I'm ready to share this version of you with anyone else."

He couldn't help the note of possession in his voice. She was Galatea to his Pygmalion, and he wanted to keep her all to himself. To explore every facet of her transformation, and then to remove each layer of her new sophistication before laying the true Margaret Cole bare to his eyes and to his hungering body.

Margaret dipped her head shyly and Will had to acknowledge the stark reminder that while, externally at least, Margaret was everything he needed in a female companion, beneath the luxurious trappings his money had provided she was still a small-town girl. Albeit a small-town girl with a magnetic appeal that threatened to scramble his wits.

He forced his lips into a smile.

"But don't worry. I'm not going to be quite so selfish as to keep you all to myself. Not this time, anyway."

"I'm pleased to hear it. I've been looking forward to dinner."

"Would you like a glass of wine before we go? I'm sure Henri will hold our table a little longer."

Margaret nodded; the movement a sensual inclination of her elegant neck. Oh, how he looked forward to exploring every inch of her starting with that spot right there in the hollow of her throat.

"I'd like that," she said.

Will stepped away from her before he did something stupid, like obey his instincts and ruffle up some of that poise she wore like a cloak around her.

"Do you like red wine? I have an excellent Pinot Noir open."

"I can't say I've tried that variety before but I'm willing to give it a go."

He picked up the bottle and poured a second glass of the bright ruby-colored liquid.

"Here," he said, handing her the goblet. "Smell it first and tell me what comes to mind."

Margaret took the glass from him, and lifted it to her nose. She closed her eyes and inhaled gently, all her senses focused on what he'd instructed her to do. Her eyes flew open.

"I can smell plums and berries. Is that right? It makes me think of summer and long lazy days."

"That's spot on. You have a good nose. Now taste it and let me know what you think."

She pressed the glass to her lower lip and tipped it gently, allowing a small sip of the beverage to enter the soft recesses of her mouth. Will felt as if he'd received a punch to his gut as he watched, totally mesmerized, while she swallowed then licked her lips. It was nothing more than a swift dart of her tongue over the plump fullness of her lower lip but it was enough to send his blood pumping through his body with a velocity that almost made him dizzy.

"It's good. I can taste the fruit now, and something else. Something woody?"

"Again, you're right. Well done."

Good grief, was his hand shaking? he thought as he reached for his own glass and took a slug of the wine he'd so anticipated only a few short minutes ago. He couldn't believe she affected him so deeply and in such a short period of time. He cast her another look. She wasn't exactly unaffected herself. There was a fine blush of color along her cheekbones that hadn't been there when she'd arrived and she certainly hadn't had enough wine to justify a flush of heat to her face.

This attraction between them was something else.

"Tell me about the rest of your day," he prompted. "I see Paige has certainly earned her fee."

Margaret filled him in on the shopping they'd done after he'd left.

"You two covered a lot of ground today. I have to say, I like the contacts," Will commented.

"I thought I'd have more trouble getting used to them but I was pleasantly surprised. Of course I haven't tried to take these out or put in a new set yet."

Margaret laughed. The sound that bubbled from her as rich and complex as the wine in his glass. His nerves were already stretched to breaking point. Desire for her clouded rational thought. He really needed to get a grip. He wanted nothing better than to keep her all to himself, all night long. But that was impossible, he reminded himself. They needed to be seen in public for the news to filter back to his parents in New York, as he knew it eventually would.

Will was startled to discover she was an amusing companion over dinner. There was a sharp intelligence to her that he'd underestimated when he'd seen the Miss Prim version of Margaret Cole in the workplace.

Everything went fine through the course of the evening until a group of several couples came into the restaurant. The men were managers who had survived Rafe's takeover of Worth Industries. One of them nodded in Will's direction, a quizzical look on his face as he studied Will's companion, until recognition dawned. Then something less pleasant and more lascivious soon followed as the man's stare traveled down the smooth ivory column of Margaret's throat and lower, to her décolletage.

An unexpected rush of possessiveness, and an urge to protect her from such shallow and insulting interest, suffused Will. He noted she'd paled under the other man's scrutiny before very calmly replacing her cup of decaffeinated coffee back onto its saucer. At first glance he wouldn't have known how the man's look had upset her, with the exception of how pale she'd grown. But now she tucked her hands into her lap where they knotted in her heavy linen napkin, twisting the fabric over and over.

He made a point of staring at the manager until the man's fixed look lifted from Margaret's chest and he slowly came around to making eye contact with Will. It didn't take much, a mere narrowing of Will's eyes, a cooling in his expression, but the guy got the message.

"Shall we go?" Will asked, eager now to remove her from prying eyes and speculation.

His actions were in direct contrast to what he thought he'd wanted. Even the interest shown in them by the chance meeting with the gossip columnist from the *Seaside Gazette* when they'd arrived hadn't drawn this overwhelming urge to shelter Margaret from unwanted interest in their so-called relationship. He hadn't stopped to consider the ramifications of this quite far enough and he made a silent vow to be more careful of her reputation in the future. While he wasn't above using her for his own purposes, he certainly didn't want to see her become the butt of gossip and innuendo in the workplace.

"Thank you, yes, I'm ready to go," Margaret replied with the new mantle of decorum she wore around her like a cloak.

The only telltale sign of her discomfort showed in the crumpled napkin she placed on the table as she rose from her seat and gathered her evening bag.

Neither of them had drunk more than a glass of wine at dinner, but Will was still glad he was using a driver for the evening. It gave him the chance to observe Margaret a little closer, to watch her mannerisms. So far today he hadn't been able to fault her, which was great as far as convincing his parents she was the real deal. They'd see through his farce in a blink if he went out with someone who lacked common courtesy and manners.

As Will handed her into the wide bench seat in the back of the limousine he caught a glimpse of lace-topped stockings before she smoothed her skirt down over her shapely thighs. Lust hit him, hard and fast. The rational side of his mind told him his reaction was no better than that of the accounts manager he'd frozen out in the restaurant. But the less rational side of him, the side that had seen Margaret at the Valentine's ball and known he'd stop at nothing to have her, reminded him he'd kept a lid on his burgeoning passion all through the exquisitely presented meal they'd enjoyed at the restaurant.

He'd been the perfect gentleman, the perfect host. But now, in the close confines of the car and with the privacy screen firmly in place, his mind ran riot on all the things he wanted to experience with Ms. Margaret Cole.

Five

Margaret sat beside Will on the cool leather seat as the car pulled smoothly away from the entrance to Jacques'. It was as if they were cocooned together in a protective bubble and she found the sensation vastly more reassuring than that moment when the manager from accounting had recognized her at the restaurant with Will. The awful assessing look in his eyes had made her feel sick to her stomach. It was exactly the kind of look she'd spent most of her life trying to avoid.

What made it worse was that his wife worked in HR, and she was an inveterate gossip. Margaret wouldn't be at all surprised to discover she was the main topic of water-cooler conversation before nine o'clock tomorrow morning.

She looked out the window at the passing scenery, but her eyes failed to register her surroundings. All she could do was silently castigate herself for being such an idiot. Who did she really think she was? She'd allowed herself to foolishly be seduced into thinking she could belong in this world. But it took far more than clothing and clever makeup to make that leap. Realistically, she was nothing but a tool in a very elaborate game designed by Will Tanner. And she'd become a shamefully eager participant.

It *had* been fun to dress up like this tonight. To allow her senses to be wooed by the glamour of the clothes she wore, the sensuality of allowing the woman she kept buried deep inside to come out. But, as much as she wished for it to be real and true, it wasn't her.

The final vestiges of the fantasy-like qualities of today's activities faded away. Tonight she had to go home, and no doubt face the silent accusations of her brother. Or not so silent, given Jason's propensity to speak his mind. She grimaced at her reflection in the glass. He wouldn't be happy with this new version of her, especially given the man who had engineered it all.

And then there was tomorrow. Work. The word echoed in her mind. She sent a silent prayer of thanks to Paige for the consideration with which she'd helped Maggie choose her new work wardrobe. While the clothing was more fitted than she usually wore, it did nothing to overly emphasize her obvious attributes. At least she wouldn't be subjected to the kind of look she'd experienced in the restaurant.

Strange how one man's gaze upon her could make her feel uncomfortable—dirty, even. Yet another's lit a slow burning fire deep inside of her that even now, beneath all her concerns, still simmered.

She started as she felt Will's warm fingers wrap around her hand where it lay in her lap. He laced his digits through hers and drew her hand to his lips, pressing a brief kiss against her knuckles.

"I'm sorry the evening had to end that way, Margaret."

"It wasn't your fault."

"No, it wasn't, but I'm angry you had to feel uncomfort for simply being you. Beautiful."

His words were like a balm to her soul, but she knew she shouldn't, couldn't, accept them.

"No, I'm not beautiful." She put up her free hand to silence him as he made to protest. "I'm not just saying that so you can argue the point with me. I know my limitations. And speaking of those limitations—" she gently withdrew her fingers from his clasp "—we have to discuss how we're going to conduct this arrangement at work."

Will eyed her carefully in the darkened compartment, his silence stretching out between them uncomfortably. Eventually, he cleared his throat and spoke, "It's simple, isn't it? You'll act as if you're both my fiancée and my executive assistant."

"But it's all so sudden, our *engagement*. Don't you think people will talk? Are you sure that's what you want?" she protested.

"No one will dare discuss our relationship behind your back, or to your face, for that matter. You can be certain of that, Margaret. I will ensure you aren't made a topic of casual discussion."

"You can't hold back human nature. People will talk."

"Not if I threaten their jobs, they won't," he growled in the darkness.

"Please don't. After you've gone back to New York I still need to be able to work with those people."

He breathed a sound of irritation before inclining his head in agreement. "Okay," he said begrudgingly. "I won't threaten anyone's job, but I will make it clear that our relationship is no one's business but our own."

Good luck with that, Margaret thought with a wry smile. "Thank you. Now, in the office? Is it to be common knowledge that we're…an item?"

"Yes," Will said, sitting up straighter as if he'd come to a decision. "I think that'll put a halt to conjecture right from the start. Which reminds me, we need to get you a ring. Damn, I should have thought of that today. People will think it's strange if you're not wearing one."

Margaret's breath caught in her throat. A ring? She hadn't even thought that far. Just the thought of what Jason would say when she arrived home with her new wardrobe was enough to send a cold chill of foreboding down her spine.

"Is that really necessary? Couldn't it wait a while? After all, everyone is going to think this is a whirlwind affair as it is."

"I want you wearing my ring for your protection if nothing else, Margaret," Will said solemnly. "No one will dare question our relationship that way. Let's stick as close to the truth as possible. If anyone asks, we can say we met at the Valentine's ball and have been seeing each other ever since, on the quiet of course, but now we've decided to bring it all out in the open. Will that cause any problems for you amongst your friends?"

Margaret thought for a few moments. Her closest friends, Gillian and Sarah, would be surprised but happy for her, provided they believed this engagement was the real deal. Jason was the only fly in the ointment. His objections were already the hardest to bear.

But she was doing this, all of this, for him. To keep his job safe. To keep him, hopefully, out of the courts and out of jail. The lingering remnants of enjoyment she'd taken out of the day soured on her tongue.

How could she have lost sight of that? How could she have let her delight—in her new look, her new wardrobe, in simply spending time with a handsome man who made her the center of his attention—overcome her responsibilities toward her brother? Her parents would be ashamed that she'd allowed herself to be so easily swayed from the seriousness of the situation she and Jason now found themselves in. *She* was ashamed.

She saw they were pulling into the driveway at the Tennis Club. She reached forward and tapped on the glass, which slid down to reveal the driver.

"Could you let me off here, please? My car's in the car park over there."

Margaret gestured toward where her car sat in isolation in the back row. The old vehicle seemingly ostracized from its shiny later-model companions parked in the next few rows. The limousine glided to a halt.

"Are you sure you don't want to stay here at the club? I can arrange a room for you if you prefer not to stay in my suite," Will said with a look in his eyes that sent a flush of warmth unfurling from the pit of her belly.

No matter how much she pilloried herself today, just one look from him was enough to start that slow melt deep inside her.

"No, I have my own home. I'd like to keep it that way."

"Have you always been this fiercely independent?" Will asked with a smile.

"Since my parents died, I suppose. It's become a habit," she admitted.

Will exited the limo ahead of her and turned to help her out.

"Maybe it's time you shared some of that load you carry," he commented.

Was he criticizing Jason? She felt herself bristle automatically in defense of her younger brother, words of justification on the tip of her tongue, before she reined herself in.

"I can manage just fine," she finally said, a little more sharply than she'd originally intended but it got the point across.

Will walked her over to her car and stood to one side as she fiddled with her key in the door lock.

"Trouble?" he inquired.

"No, it's okay. It just requires a bit of finesse to get it to work," she said as the key finally engaged with the tumblers inside and the door unlocked.

"I suppose you have all today's shopping in there, too?"

"Yes."

"A bit risky given how easy your car would be to break in to."

Will's comment stung. So what if she didn't have one of the latest models off the production lines of American driving excellence.

"I would have thought the security here at the Tennis Club would ensure that my parcels are quite safe. Besides, they're in the trunk so it's not as if anyone can see them on display."

"No, but anyone could have seen you put them in there, and it's not as if it would take someone with a MENSA-rated IQ to figure a way into your car," Will pressed. "I don't like the idea of your security being so easily compromised. Tomorrow I'll see you have another car to use." At her gasp of shock he continued, "Don't argue with me, Margaret. I need you to have something reliable to get you to and from work and other appointments you'll be undertaking with me. It makes sense that I put a car at your disposal."

Margaret couldn't think of a single argument that would sway him. Will stepped forward and tipped her chin up with one finger.

"Are you angry with me now?" he asked.

Conscious of their audience, the driver still waiting for Will in the limousine that idled a short distance away, Margaret shook her head. She wasn't angry, exactly. But there was a sense of frustration that he'd put her in a position where she couldn't refuse. A sense of frustration that was spilling over in all areas of her life with the power and force of a tidal wave.

"Looks like I'll have to remedy that, won't I?"

Before she could summon a protest Will kissed her—his lips gentle, yet persuasive. A tiny sigh of capitulation eased from her throat and he took the action as an opportunity to deepen their embrace. Without realizing what she was doing, Margaret wound her arms over his shoulders, the fingers of one hand driving into his short hair and cupping the back of his head as if she couldn't quite get enough of him.

When his tongue brushed against hers she felt her body ignite. She leaned into him, pressing her breasts against the hardness of his chest, letting her hips roll against his in a silent dance of torment.

And then, just like that, he broke contact. As if he'd proven his point that no matter what she did, or thought, or said, she was his for the taking. Whenever and however he wanted her. It should have galled her to realize it, but instead she worked on trying to calm the thrumming desire that wound through her.

"Sweet dreams," he whispered against her mouth. "I will see you in the morning."

She nodded and got into her car, her hand trembling a little as she fitted the key to the ignition and fired the car to life. Will pushed her door closed and stood to one side as she backed out and began to drive away. A flick of her eyes to her rearview mirror confirmed he stayed there, watching her, until she hit the driveway that led to the main road.

She had no idea how she was going to handle this overwhelming effect he had upon her. None at all. While every cell in her body bade her to give in to it, to him, logic told her that it would only lead to heartbreak—her heartbreak.

* * *

She'd slept surprisingly well after the turmoil in which she'd ended her evening. Thankfully, Jason had been in his room, the lights off but the sounds of his TV filtering through the closed door. She hadn't wanted to disturb him. Hadn't wanted to face his recriminations—especially when he saw the number of bags she'd brought in from her car.

Now, all she had to do was decide on what to wear to work today. She skimmed her hand over the hangers in her wardrobe before settling on a 1940s-inspired dress with a deep collared V-neck and three-quarter sleeves. The large black and white hounds-tooth pattern of the fabric drew attention to the design of the dress, rather than the person wearing it, and she and Paige had been in total agreement about it the second she'd stepped out of the dressing room. A wide black belt at her waist finished it off and after brushing her hair and applying a light coating of makeup, Margaret went through to the kitchen.

To her surprise, Jason was already there.

"You were late home last night," he said as she reached for the carafe and poured herself a mug of coffee. "Work late at the office?"

"No, I had dinner out. I didn't disturb you when I came in, did I?"

He barked an ironic laugh. "Disturb me? Well, that all depends on who you had dinner with, doesn't it?"

"Why would it depend on that?"

"You were with him, weren't you? And look at you this morning. That's new. Did he buy it?"

Margaret flinched at the accusation in Jason's voice. She drew in a leveling breath and chose her words carefully.

"Mr. Tanner and I agreed that my old wardrobe was perhaps lacking a little for my new role. He very kindly offered to rectify that."

"Your new role, huh? And what exactly is that role to be, Maggie? How long before he has you warming his sheets?"

"How dare you speak to me like that?" she flung back. "I'm not like that and you know it."

"Yeah, but the sister I know doesn't stay away from her desk at work all day long, doesn't ignore her cell phone and doesn't sneak in late at night trying to avoid me, either."

Her cell phone. Oh, God, she hadn't even thought to check it all day and she'd been so rattled by the time she got home it hadn't even occurred to check it then.

"Did you need me for something?" she asked as calmly as she could.

"That's not the point. You're not behaving like yourself. What's going on?"

Margaret chewed at her lower lip. How was she going to approach this without aggravating the tenuous thread she and her brother had between them at the moment?

"I'm sorry. I was distracted."

"By him."

Jason spoke the two words as if they were poison on his tongue.

"Yes, by him. But, Jason, I only took this job to keep *your* job safe. I know you don't like it but that's the way it is. We can't afford for either of us to lose our jobs. You know as well as I do that working for Cameron Enterprises is the only thing keeping our heads above water."

"I don't like it, Maggie. He's only been in your sphere for two days and already he's changing you. It's not just your clothes, but your hair and…" He peered closer at her face. "Are you wearing contacts? What's with that? Weren't you good enough for him the way you were?"

"As his fiancée I'll be expected to look a certain way. I could hardly argue when he covered the bill for everything."

"Everything? So I expect we won't be seeing any more serviceable white cotton in the laundry?"

Jason snorted, the sound grating on Margaret's nerves. Oh, it was all so easy for him, wasn't it? To sit in judgment of her when she was doing this for him. If he hadn't been tempted... A slow-building anger began to well inside her. She'd done her best all these years and it was never going to be enough. Well, it was time he faced some truths.

"Keep your mind out of the gutter for once, Jason, and try to focus on someone that isn't yourself."

The sharpness of her voice made him sit up in his chair, a look of surprise on his face. Never, not even when he'd been a sulky teenager, delivered home by the local police, had she spoken to him this way. She forced herself to soften her tone. It wouldn't serve any purpose to antagonize him, anyway.

"Look, William Tanner and I are, for all intents and purposes, engaged."

"You're mad. No one is going to believe it."

"They'll have to." Maggie crossed her fingers behind her back and hoped for the strength to get herself through this. "If anyone asks you can tell them that we've been seeing each on the quiet for almost two months and it's...it's become something a lot bigger than either of us expected.

"The news will no doubt be all around the office today, we were seen out at dinner last night together and a reporter from the *Gazette* was there, too. We have to keep our stories straight about this, Jason, before the gossip mongers get ahold of it."

"Well, don't expect me to welcome him here with open arms. I can't stand the man."

"I know. And don't worry. I won't be bringing him here."

"So you'll be going to him. You'll be at his beck and call at work and on your own time?"

His words couldn't be more true but she couldn't tell him the truth.

"That's right, and that's my choice, Jason. A choice I made for us both. Remember that."

And it was her choice. One she wished she'd never been pushed into making, but there was no going back now.

Six

"I've got tickets to a live show tonight. Are you interested? We can head into San Diego after work and I thought we could stay over—make a weekend of it. How much time do you need to pack a bag?"

Margaret sat up straight in her chair, her hands stilling on the keyboard where she'd been typing up a report for Will. They'd been working together for three days, excluding the day he'd taken her shopping, and every night they'd had dinner together either in his suite or in one of the multitude of restaurants dotted along the coast. Each night he'd done no more than kiss her good-night, and each night she'd gone home, her body aching for more. To all appearances they were very much the engaged couple but, for Margaret, it was growing more difficult each day to separate the truth from reality—even with Jason's brooding silences and fulminous looks when they crossed paths at home.

A weekend solely in Will's company? The idea both thrilled

and terrified her in equal proportions. Jason would be scathing, she had no doubt. But the prospect of spending forty-eight hours alone with Will Tanner was infinitely preferable to the stifling atmosphere at home—for more reasons than one. She'd no sooner had the thought than she instantly felt disloyal. It wasn't Jason's fault he was so unhappy. But why should they both be miserable? Margaret took a deep breath and answered.

"I'd love to go. When do you need me to be ready?"

"If you're finished with that report you could head home now and I'll pick you up in," he flicked a look at the understated yet expensive watch he wore on one wrist, "say two hours. That'll give us plenty of time to drive in, check into the hotel and have a bite of something to eat. The show starts at eight and we can have a late supper afterward."

"Do you want me to take care of the hotel bookings?" she asked, reaching for her phone.

"Already done," Will said, meeting her gaze for the first time.

There was something in his eyes that made her forget what she was doing and her hand hovered, outstretched over her telephone, before she realized what she was doing and pulled it back. Snapping back to reality didn't change anything, though. If anything it made the sudden pulse of excitement that swelled through her all the more overwhelming. Had he arranged one room, or two? She'd find out soon enough.

She forced herself to break the silent, loaded connection between them and turned her head toward her computer screen. A quick flick of her fingers over the keyboard and the document was sent to the printer.

"I'll be ready to leave in a few minutes. Do you need my address?" she asked with as much composure as she could muster.

"No, I have all your details."

Not surprising, given his investigation of her and Jason. The reminder should have been a wake-up call for her to get her head out of the clouds but she chose to ignore the frisson of warning that infiltrated her overheated mind.

They were going away together for the night. Away from the prying eyes of the office. Away from the simmering resentment that clouded every conversation she had with her brother. Just the thought of it was enough to make her feel lighter, happier.

It only took a few minutes to check the printed report, then copy and bind it for the meeting Will had organized for Monday morning. She locked the reports away in her cabinet and let Will know she was on her way home.

Not even the spiteful comment from one of the accounting staff that reached her ears on her way out the door, about it being nice to be the boss's fiancée and be able to leave early on a Friday, was enough to take the polish off the hours ahead.

By the time she heard Will's knock at the door of her home she was ready. The April afternoon had turned quite cool after the spring sunshine of earlier in the day and, as a result, she'd probably packed far too many clothes but, she consoled herself, better too much than not quite enough.

She swung open the front door and her breath caught fast in her chest. She hadn't seen Will dressed casually before, at least not in anything like the green-gray sweater he was wearing now with a pair of sinfully sexy jeans. Words failed her as her eyes took in the subtle breadth of his shoulders and the way the sweater fit snugly across his chest. The lean strength visible beneath the ribbed woolen knit made her mouth dry and she swallowed hard.

"All ready?" Will asked, his mouth quirking up in a half smile.

"Well, I'm all packed," she said, gesturing to the small

suitcase she had standing in the compact entrance to the house.

"Shall we head off then?"

"Sure, just let me check I've locked everything up securely first."

Margaret shot around the house, double-checking all the doors and windows were closed and that the note she'd left for Jason was where he wouldn't miss it. By the time she swung her key in the deadlock of the front door, Will had already put her case in the trunk of his midnight-blue Chrysler 300 and was waiting by the passenger door for her to come outside.

"Sorry to keep you waiting," she said, suddenly shy.

It was ridiculous to feel this way, she told herself. They'd been working together the past week in close quarters, and had spent several hours together outside of work as well. She'd gotten to know him as a man of integrity, quite at odds with the hard-ass attitude he'd been painted with when he'd first arrived for the takeover. He struck her as being fully committed to finding the most workable solution to the transition of ownership from the Worth family to Rafe Cameron. Will was intelligent and insightful. Both qualities Margaret admired greatly.

She'd had plenty of time to think about her earlier perceptions of Will, in particular, plenty of time to *re*think her perceptions. He could easily have let Jason go to the wall over the funds that had been so artfully skimmed. Sure, he'd thrown his weight around a bit to get her to agree to act as his fiancée as well, but over dinner last night he'd told her a bit about the reasons behind his need for her helping him. In particular, he told her about the family farm his grandparents had run—the fifth generation of his family to do so—and his father's plans to sell the property if Will couldn't satisfy his wish for his youngest son to settle down.

She'd seen a side of him that no one at the office had seen

before. Certainly a side that no one expected to see from him. By all accounts the whole farming operation was huge and Will's dad was keen to make the most of international interest and sell to the highest bidder. But Will was equally determined the property should remain in family hands— specifically his hands. He'd talked about what the time he'd spent on the farm growing up had meant to him, how it had helped him keep a perspective in life as his parents' wealth had grown in leaps and bounds. His father had never wanted to take over the farm, as had generations of Tanners before him, choosing instead a career in finance. Albert Tanner's acumen had eventually led to him taking a senior management role in New York that had seen the whole family relocate to the other side of the world.

But deep down, Will still felt it was vitally important to maintain that link with his family's past. The reminder that generations of Tanners had hewn a living from what had sometimes been a hostile land, and in bitter conditions, yet had managed to hold on to humor and each other through it all. While he had no plans to actively farm the land himself, he saw no reason why the current method of using a caretaker/manager, with a full complement of staff, couldn't be maintained. And if he was so inclined as to visit every now and then, and muck in with the rest of them, then so be it.

The thought of Will in a pair of muddy rubber work boots—what had he called them? Gumboots?—and sturdy farm gear brought a small smile to her face.

"Penny for them?" Will said, interrupting her thoughts.

"Just thinking about what you told me last night and trying to picture you in a pair of gumboots," she said, a gurgle of laughter rippling from her throat. "Seriously, after seeing you day in, day out in your suits, it's quite a stretch of the imagination."

Will grinned at her briefly before transferring his attention back to the traffic winding in front of them on the freeway.

"Believe it, it happens."

The trip south into San Diego went smoothly, taking no more than half an hour and before Margaret even had time to fully appreciate their downtown surroundings, they were pulling up in front of one of the city's historic five-star hotels and her car door was being opened by liveried staff.

Her heart was in her mouth as they stepped into the grand lobby. She'd never seen anything like it in her life. Crystal chandeliers hung from the ceiling and muted-tone silk carpets made her fear to tread upon them.

"You like it?" Will asked at her side.

"Like doesn't even begin to describe it."

"Wait until you see our suite."

A suite. That could mean two bedrooms, couldn't it? Margaret wasn't sure if she felt a sense of relief, or regret. She didn't have too long to find out, though. They were checked in with supreme courtesy and efficiency and before long were shown to a suite comprising two levels.

While Will tipped the bellboy, Margaret made an exploratory tour. The lower level was made up of a sitting room which opened out onto a wide, furnished balcony. She shook her head slightly. Even the outdoor furniture put that of her humble home to shame. If she hadn't been aware of the two different worlds in which she and Will moved before, she certainly was now. She carried on through the suite and made her way up the staircase, her hand trailing on the black walnut railing.

At the top of the stairs was the master bedroom. Perhaps the door off to one side led to another bedroom, she thought, as she turned the handle and exposed a decadently luxurious marble bathroom. She pulled the door closed again and turned around.

One bed.

One huge, luxurious bed covered in soft pillows and fine bed linens.

Her nerves jangled. It wasn't as if she hadn't spent most of her waking hours during the past week imagining what it would be like to be in Will's arms—in his bed. But facing the potential reality was another thing entirely. Was she even ready for this? In so many ways, no, she most definitely wasn't. However, from deep within her a voice grew stronger, its response to her internal question a resounding "yes." He'd said he wouldn't have to force her, and he'd been so very right.

Will waited on the lower level of the suite as Margaret investigated what the rooms had to offer. Had she noticed he'd only booked one bedroom yet? he wondered. It had been a conscious decision on his part, although if she demurred he had no problem with booking a separate room for her. But it was time he took their so-called relationship to the next level. She was comfortable with him now, physically and socially, although if she was going to convince his parents she really was his fiancée, he needed her to be totally invested in him. He'd hoped to take his time seducing her, but an email from his mother this week had mentioned his father was sourcing realtors in New Zealand who specialized in rural property.

To delay any longer would be cutting things a little too close and he wasn't prepared to take the risk.

He looked up as Margaret made her way back down the staircase to the sitting room.

"Some champagne?" he asked, gesturing to the ice bucket, sweating gracefully on a linen placemat on the coffee table.

She hesitated. Was the objection to their sleeping arrangements going to come now? Will held his breath until she appeared to make up her mind and crossed the room to his side.

"Why not? That would be a lovely way to start the weekend."

He relaxed. Everything was going to plan quite nicely. With deft movements he dispensed with the foil and cage at the neck of the champagne bottle and popped the cork before spilling the sparkling golden liquid into the crystal champagne flutes on the table. He picked them both up and offered one to Margaret.

"To us," he said.

She met his gaze with a serious look in her dark eyes. "To us," she answered and tapped her glass gently against his.

Without breaking their visual connection he lifted his glass to his lips and took a sip. She mirrored his actions, all the time her eyes holding his, and he felt the desire that he'd kept tightly coiled within him all week begin to unravel and take life.

When she took her glass away from her mouth a slight shimmer of moisture remained there. Tempting him. Daring him. He took her glass from her unprotesting hand and placed it back on the table with his own. When he straightened he reached for her, drawing her to him as if the action had been predestined. If he stopped to think about it, it had been— certainly from the moment she'd chosen to protect her brother and his job. But it wasn't time for thinking anymore. No, now it was time to act.

As his lips sealed hers he both felt and heard her surrender to him. It had been the same each time he'd kissed her this past week. The tiny hum she made. It intoxicated him in a way no other stimulant ever could. His whole body focused on the sound, every nerve in his body taut with anticipation.

Her arms tightened around him, as if she could hardly support herself without him, and her kiss was as open and giving as he'd hoped for. He adored the taste of her, the texture of her. It was all he could do to hold on to his wits, to remind himself that this seduction should progress by degrees, not flame out in a flashover of uncontrolled need. But try as he might, his body demanded more. And it demanded it now.

Will reluctantly broke the kiss, noting with pleasure the tiny moue of regret on her lips. He took her hand and led her to the staircase and slowly drew her up the stairs. At the top he took her into his arms again, and this time he didn't plan to let go for quite some time.

The buttons on the silk blouse she wore slid free with ease, and he feasted his gaze upon her soft, smooth skin. Fine white lace cupped her generous breasts and as much as he admired the craftsmanship of the undergarment, it obstructed his view of her just a little too much. He slid her blouse from her shoulders and free of her arms, absorbing her tiny cries with his mouth as he trailed his fingertips over her softly rounded arms, chasing the piece of clothing until it fell to the floor.

All week she'd tormented him with her wardrobe that hinted at, yet concealed, her feminine curves. She was the most sensuously put together woman he'd ever met, yet the most modest at the same time. The juxtaposition was both intriguing and provocative. And now she was all his to discover.

It took the merest twist of the hooks at the back of her bra and her glorious breasts were revealed to him. He smoothed his hands across her ribcage, bringing them underneath the full creamy-skinned globes and cupping them gently, reverently. She gasped as he brushed his thumbs across the deep rose pink tips, feeling them pebble into tight buds beneath his touch.

He trailed small kisses from the corner of her mouth to her jaw as he relished the weight and firmness of her in his hands. When he bent his head lower and caught a tender tip gently between his teeth, a small keening sound broke from Margaret's throat. He hesitated, laving the areola with the tip of his tongue, waiting for her to tell him to stop, but instead he felt her fingers drive into his hair and cup the back of his head, holding him there.

A tremor of satisfaction rippled through him. She wanted this as much as he did. She wouldn't regret a second of it, he promised silently. Not one single moment. He would give and give until there was nothing left.

Later, he couldn't say how they came to be naked and lying together on the bed, flesh burning with heat and need for one another. The details were unimportant. But several things would remain in Will's memory forever.

The way his hands trembled as he explored the dips and hollows of Margaret's lush body. Her unabashed joy in his touch. Her sharp sigh of completion as he brought her to orgasm, the taste of her as he did so. And then, the overwhelming sensation of entering her body, of feeling her clamp her inner strength around him, of drawing her to yet another peak before he tumbled past reason and joined her on that plane where they both hovered, suspended by pleasure, before slowly returning back to reality.

They lay there for some time, legs still entwined, hearts still racing, fingers still tracing one another before Will could put together a single rational thought.

He'd lost track of whether he was the seducer or the seduced. Something had happened while they made love. It had ceased to be something he wanted to do, albeit it had been a task he'd relished. No, somewhere along the line it had become something bigger than that. Something more. Something he didn't want to examine too closely—certainly not now while he had so very much at stake.

And that's what he needed to concentrate on now, he reminded himself. They still had plenty of time before they needed to get ready for the show tonight. It didn't start until eight, and he had plenty of ideas of how they could fill their time until then.

Margaret basked in a rosy glow of supreme satisfaction as they exited the theater. Will had been amazingly attentive all evening so far, and he was an incredibly considerate lover, too. Not that she had a great deal to compare him to, but no one had ever brought her to the heights of pleasure he had. Her arm was tucked through Will's and she felt her sensitized breast brush against his arm as they made their way outside through the press of theater patrons. Even through his suit fabric she could feel the heat of his body, and felt the answering burn of her own.

She'd barely been able to concentrate on the performance of *Fiddler on the Roof,* even though the story was one she'd adored since childhood. All evening she'd been excruciatingly aware of the man at her side. The man who'd bared her for his delectation only a few short hours earlier, when they'd finally gotten around to finishing their champagne, amidst more lovemaking.

If she was a cat she'd be purring right now. It wasn't until her vision was blinded by a sudden bright flash that Margaret became aware they were no longer caught in the throng of bodies exiting the theater, but stood upon the pavement waiting for the car and driver the hotel had arranged for them earlier.

"Don't worry," Will murmured in her ear as she looked around to see where the flash had come from. "It's just some paparazzo looking for some celebrity gossip."

"Well, they won't find much from us, will they?"

"I don't know. The way you look tonight they'll probably print the picture to sell more papers."

Margaret pushed playfully against his chest. "You have to be kidding."

But Will's eyes grew serious as he looked back at her, the smile fading from his face. "Oh, no, I'm not kidding at all. You look sensational."

"Well, if I do, it's all because of you. You made me this way."

Their car materialized through the traffic and pulled up smoothly alongside of them. Will didn't answer, and opened the back door for her to get in ahead of him. Had she hit a sore point? she wondered, as he followed her into the car and they drew away from the curb.

"Hungry?" Will asked.

Margaret realized she was famished. The light snacks they'd eventually brought up to the bed and enjoyed with the balance of their champagne had tided her over but now she was ready for something more substantial.

"Definitely," she said.

"Then it's just as well I've booked us somewhere for supper," he said with a wink.

She looked at him across the semidarkness of the car interior and felt her chest constrict. There was something about him that appealed to her on every level—had from the first moment she'd seen him—and it deepened with every minute she spent with him now.

By the time they were seated at the intimately lit restaurant Will had chosen, Margaret felt as if every cell in her body was attuned to his. She left the menu selection to him, preferring instead to watch him as he perused the choices available to them. He approached their order with the same level of concentration he approached everything. She felt her womb clench in anticipation as she acknowledged he'd applied the same concentration to her and no doubt would again.

She slipped her foot from one expensive high-heeled

shoe and slid her foot up the inside of his calf, secure in the knowledge that no one could see her action beneath the floor-length tablecloth. He didn't so much as flinch, until her toe traced the inside of his thigh—an area she already knew he found incredibly sensitive.

His eyes flicked up to hers and in their sherry brown depths she saw raw hunger reflected there.

"I thought you said you were hungry," Will said, his voice low.

"I am. Very hungry."

She let her foot travel a little higher, until she felt the hardened ridge of his arousal. She pressed against him, smiling as he shifted slightly in his seat. She felt uncharacteristically powerful. She brought about this reaction in him and now she had his undivided attention.

"Do we have time to eat?" he asked.

"Oh, yes, but let's make it quick."

"I promise you, supper will be quick. But as to the rest of the evening…" His voice trailed off as she pressed against him again. "I think I may need to make you pay for this, Margaret Cole."

"I think I'm up for it," she teased, smiling back at him. "Are you?"

"As if there's any question."

His hand shot under the table and captured her foot, his thumb massaging firmly against the arch. She never knew feet could be such an erogenous zone. She was all but a melted puddle of heat and longing.

He released her foot, giving it a soft pat before gently pushing it away.

"I have something for you," he said as he reached into the pocket of his jacket.

"No, Will. Seriously, you've already given me too much."

He shook his head. "This is a very necessary part of our agreement, Margaret."

She stilled. The illusion that she'd foolishly allowed herself to build faded away in increments. She composed herself, damming back the joy she'd indulged in and reminded herself that their whole relationship was merely a pretense.

"Give me your left hand," he instructed as he flipped open the distinctive blue jewelry box.

She couldn't see what he hid inside it but held out her hand as he'd asked.

"Close your eyes," he said, a note of teasing in his voice.

Margaret again did as he'd asked and waited. Her heart jumped a little as his warm fingers captured hers and as she felt the cool slide of metal on her ring finger.

"There, a perfect fit. Do you like it?"

Will continued to hold her hand and as Margaret opened her eyes, they widened in shock at the stunning ring he'd placed upon her finger. Shafts of brilliance spun from the emerald-cut diamonds flanking a large rectangular glowing ruby. The gold band itself was very simple, leaving all its glory to the stones set upon it.

"It's the most beautiful thing I've ever seen," Margaret said, sudden tears springing to her eyes.

More than anything in the world right now, she wished this was for real. That the man opposite her at the table was indeed in love with her and pledging his life to hers. She blinked back the moisture and summoned all the composure she could find.

"I'll take great care of it, I promise you," she said, withdrawing her hand from his.

"It was harder to find than I thought," Will admitted. "But as soon as I saw it, I knew it was you."

His words were like tiny shards of glass tearing at her

dreams. She'd slid into the fantasy of being his fiancée with all too much ease and she needed to remind herself of the truth—that she was simply a means to an end.

Seven

Monday morning saw the return to routine that Margaret craved. Here, in the office, she could focus one hundred percent of her energy on her work. Will was away in meetings all day that day and after the intensity of the weekend, she was all too glad for the space that provided her.

Today she was looking forward to seeing one of her dearest friends, Sarah Richards, for lunch. Although they'd been four years apart at school, never really crossing paths, they'd formed a firm friendship over gallons of coffee in the intervening years. Margaret had been surprised when Sarah had married Quentin Dobbs—she hadn't really thought him Sarah's type at all, despite his long-standing crush on her— but they'd made it all work only to have it ripped apart when he was killed in a motor vehicle accident three years ago. Margaret had always admired Sarah's "take no prisoners" attitude, a legacy of her fiery red hair, she supposed. Sarah worked as a waitress in the restaurant at the Tennis Club and

Margaret had actively steered William from dining there with her. It was one thing to lie to the rest of the world about their engagement, but to one of her best friends?

But Sarah wouldn't be put off. She'd left a message on Margaret's mobile phone, saying she was free for lunch today and could meet her on the Cameron Enterprises campus. Margaret couldn't think of a single decent reason to postpone the inevitable any longer. She checked herself in the polished reflection of the elevator doors as she traveled downstairs to meet her friend. Yes, she'd pass muster. No one could tell just by looking at her that she'd just indulged in the most decadent and sensual weekend of her entire life.

"Oh, my God! You look fabulous!" Sarah gushed the instant she saw her. "What have you been up to? Actually, on second thought, maybe you shouldn't tell me, I'll only get jealous."

Margaret felt her cheeks flush with embarrassment. "Sarah, I'm still the same old me." She laughed uncomfortably.

"Well, yes, I know that. But, wow, I really like what you've done. Seriously, you look amazing. And there's more. You're glowing. It's a man, isn't it? Tell me everything. Gillian said you've been reported on in the *Gazette* as being the mystery woman on the arm of a certain Cameron Enterprises executive, is that true?" Sarah demanded, her green eyes flashing with curiosity. "Although I'm not sure I should forgive you for leaving me to *read* about your love life."

"Over lunch, I promise." Margaret laughed. "Where do you want to eat?"

"How about outside? It's warm enough and I brought a couple of roast beef subs and diet sodas. Sound good?"

Relief flooded Margaret that at least they'd be able to enjoy each other's company in the relative privacy of the campus gardens, without others straining to overhear what she was saying. It felt as if everyone wanted to know her business since her engagement to Will had become common knowledge around the office. Even more so since she'd arrived at work this morning wearing his ring.

"Sounds excellent, thanks."

After they'd settled on a bench Sarah divvied out their lunch. She sighed with unabashed pleasure as she bit into her sub. After she'd chewed and swallowed she turned to Margaret.

"So, he's good in bed, isn't he?" Sarah came straight to the point.

Margaret nearly choked on her sip of soda. "I beg your pardon?"

"He has to be brilliant, seriously. Everything about you is radiant. And look at how you're dressed. I bet he can't keep his hands off you. Who is it?"

Margaret took a deep breath. "William Tanner."

"You're kidding me. The CFO from Cameron Enterprises? One of Rafe's henchmen?"

"The one and only," Margaret conceded wryly.

Sarah sat back against the back of the bench and took stock of her friend. Margaret knew the exact instant her eyes picked up the ring on her finger.

"*You're engaged to him?* And you didn't tell me?"

Sarah grabbed her hand and turned it this way and that in the light, gasping over the beauty of the stones.

"It's all very sudden," Margaret said. "It's taken me by surprise as well."

"You guys haven't known each other very long, are you sure about this? It's not like you to rush into things."

Margaret struggled to find the right words. Words that wouldn't come across as a blatant lie. Finding the balance between the truth and what would satisfy her very astute friend was not going to be easy.

"It's different from anything else I've experienced," she

finally managed. "We met back in February—you remember me telling you about that kiss at the Valentine's Day ball?"

Sarah nodded, the expression on her face silently urging Margaret to continue.

"Well, it kind of grew from there. We just went to San Diego for the weekend. It was out of this world."

Suitably distracted from having to delve into the whys and wherefores of the engagement, Margaret told Sarah about the weekend she and Will had just shared.

"Well," Sarah said, when Margaret had finished, "I'm really happy for you. You deserve someone special. You've put your own needs on the backburner for far too long. It's time you looked after yourself first."

Margaret swallowed back the guilt that came hard on the heels of her friend's words. It wasn't fair to deceive her like this—to deceive anyone, for that matter—but to save Jason's job she had to keep the truth very firmly locked deep inside.

"Thanks, Sarah. So, anyway, that's enough about me. Tell me, how's your grandmother doing?"

Sarah laughed. "You know Grandma Kat. She's great. She's already roped me in to helping plan her birthday party in a couple of months' time. Like she even needs the help!"

Margaret let Sarah's conversation wash over her and breathed a sigh of relief that she had been diverted from Margaret's engagement being the topic "du jour." It was a few minutes before she realized that Sarah was waiting for her to answer something.

"I'm sorry, what did you say?" Margaret asked apologetically.

"Apology accepted," Sarah said with an exasperated smile. "Too busy reliving that weekend of yours, I suppose. Can't say I blame you. Anyway, I just noticed that guy over there.

Does he look familiar to you? I feel like I should know him from somewhere."

Margaret looked across the gardens at the tall cowboy walking along the path toward the main building. In amongst all the suits he stood out, and not in a bad way. She looked a little harder. There was definitely something familiar about the way he looked, even the way he moved, but she couldn't pin him down.

"I know what you mean." Margaret shrugged. "I can't place him, though. Maybe he has a double out there. They say we all do."

"Hmm, yeah," Sarah said before looking at her wristwatch. "Oh, my, look at the time. I really have to go. I have an early start to my shift this evening and a ton of stuff to do before then. It's been great to see you again. Don't leave it so long next time, okay?"

Margaret embraced her friend and took solace in the warmth of Sarah's unabashed hug. She ached to tell her the truth. To share it with the one person who'd probably understand better than most just why she was doing what she was doing. But she knew she couldn't.

"I won't. And you take care."

"Always do." Sarah stood and started to gather up their trash.

"Leave that. You brought it, the least I can do is clean up. Thanks again for lunch."

"No problem. Your turn next time." Sarah grinned back at her. "See you soon, yeah?"

"Definitely."

Margaret gave a small wave as Sarah headed off toward the car park. For a minute she sat back on the bench and closed her eyes against the brightness of the sun burning high in the clear blue sky. Being with Sarah had been a breath of fresh air. But now she had to get back to business—and back to the business of continuing to be the best counterfeit fiancée Will Tanner could ever want.

Margaret was exhausted by the time she let herself into the front door at home. It had been a busy day and, to her chagrin, she'd missed Will's presence in the office far more than she'd anticipated. It both irritated and surprised her. It wasn't as if they really were engaged, or as if they actually meant anything to one another.

"Not out with the boss man tonight?"

Jason's voice made her start.

"No," she replied carefully. "How was your day?"

"As good as it gets when you have a hundred sets of eyes watching your every move," he said bitterly.

Margaret sighed. So it was going to be like that. She'd hoped that maybe they could have a nice quiet evening together. Catch a movie on cable and just enjoy one another's company like they used to. Like before this whole business with Will Tanner.

"At least you still have your job. It could be worse, you know."

Jason snorted a laugh that totally lacked a spark of humor. "Sure, although not by much."

"Hey, why don't we put Cameron Enterprises behind us for a night," Margaret suggested. "Sit down, order in some dinner and watch some movies together."

"Can't," Jason said, tugging on his jacket which he'd snagged from the couch in front of him.

"How come?"

"Overtime."

"Overtime? Really? I would have thou—"

"Thought what? That because I'm under supervision that they don't want me there any more than I need to be?"

"Jason, that's not—"

"I don't care what you think, Maggie. Right now I just don't want to be around you."

Her gasp of hurt split the air between them. She watched, stunned with the emotional pain that reverberated through her, as Jason closed his eyes for a couple of seconds and heaved a sigh that seemed to come from Methuselah himself.

"Ah, hell, Maggie. I'm sorry. I don't want to hurt you. I mean, I know it's ridiculous to feel this way. You're my sister and you've looked after me better than anyone else ever could. Given me opportunities that Mom and Dad always wanted me to have. You've even kept the house exactly the way they left it. Sometimes it feels like a freaking shrine to our old life before they died—and most of the time that's okay, it's something solid that we have in common. But sometimes it's suffocating and right now, looking at you—seeing the way you've changed for *him,* seeing how happy you are—it's just more than I can stand."

She crossed the room and put her hand on his arm. "It doesn't have to be like this, Jason. He's a good man. I've seen a side of him that's different from what everyone else sees— you should see how much he has contributed personally to Hannah's Hope. He wrote a check today that was huge. Sure, he's intense and driven, but he's just and loyal, too."

"Just? You can still say that after what he's done to me?"

"Jason, I saw the reports."

"Oh, sure, that figures. You'd believe a bunch of words and numbers before you'd believe me."

"I hardly have any cause for blind loyalty, Jason," she protested. "I don't even know if I got this job on my own merits or because he wanted to keep an eye on me because of what he believed *you'd* done!"

"Oh, so now that's my fault, too. Well, sis, I don't see you protesting very hard. After all, look at you. Look at yourself.

Look at what you wear now. You'd never have been seen dead in that stuff before. You don't even drive your own car."

"So you're mad at me for wanting to look nice? For needing a vehicle that's more reliable?"

"You always looked nice—if anyone ever bothered to go beneath the surface of what you hid behind. I'm not stupid. I know you did it deliberately. And I know you haven't upgraded your car because we've been paying off my loans. But seriously, Maggie, you're so dolled up now I don't even recognize my sister inside you anymore." He snatched his arm away from her hold. "You know, I can take the changes, I can even take that you're working for that arrogant SOB, but what hurts the most is that you believe him over me. Your own brother."

Before her very eyes Jason appeared to age, looking every one of his twenty-four years, and more.

"Jason, I know it must have been tempting, but you've been given another chance."

"When will you understand, Maggie? I. Didn't. Do. It."

He turned sharply away from her and headed straight for the front door.

"Wait, please!" she cried, moving to block him. Anything to make him stay. Make him understand. "I love you, Jason. You're my brother. I've always been there for you, you know that."

"Not anymore," he said bitterly, grief stark on his face. "But when I prove that I'm right and your precious Mr. Tanner is wrong, maybe you'll believe me again."

The door slammed resoundingly behind him. Margaret stood there for some time, hoping against hope that he'd be straight back, but through the thick slab of wood she heard him start up his motorbike and head out onto the street.

On unsteady legs she made her way to her bedroom and sank onto her neatly made bed. Was Jason right? Was she struggling so hard to hold on to everything they had before their parents died that she was stifling him? She'd fought so hard to hold on to him, to prevent him from being taken into foster care.

Margaret looked up at the bedroom wall, at the map of the world covered with red pins marking all the countries she wanted to visit one day, and with a single yellow pin marking where she'd been. Here. Vista Del Mar, California.

She'd sacrificed her own dreams of education and travel to ensure that Jason had the most stable upbringing he possibly could with both their parents gone. She'd given it up without so much as a thought or regret for what might have been. She'd done it because she had to, needed to. Because it was what their parents would have expected of her. Because she loved her brother.

Slowly she got up from the bed and crossed to the wall, then slowly, painstakingly, began to remove the pins from the map. Once they were all gone and tucked back in the box from which they'd come, she took the poster off her wall and systematically tore it in two, then in two again. Then and only then did she let go of the grief that now built with steady pressure in her chest.

Nothing mattered. Not a single thing she'd done. Ever. She'd failed her brother and now she was in a relationship with a man who thought only in terms of profit and loss. Hell, it wasn't even a real relationship. It was a farce perpetuated so he could trick his father into signing over ownership of something that should, by right, have been his all along.

Margaret knew she would continue to do whatever it took for Will to have what was his. She'd given her word and that word was gold. And, in the past week, she'd seen a different side to the man they'd all said was unflinchingly ruthless. A side that spoke to her on a level she'd never anticipated.

She'd shared intimacies with him this weekend she'd never

shared with another man. Been lifted to heights of pleasure that were as addictive as they were seductive. She'd felt special and cherished—as if she were half of a pair that belonged together—and, damn it, she wanted it all again.

Margaret fisted the torn poster between her hands and threw the balled-up mass to one corner of the room, before collapsing on her bed—sobbing now as if her heart would break. A heart that she now knew belonged irrevocably to a man who didn't return her feelings. A man whose world was so far removed from her own reality that she felt like a fairy-tale princess when she moved within it.

But the clock was ticking fast toward midnight. Once Will had what he needed she'd be redundant to him, in more ways than one. As redundant as it now appeared she was to Jason as well. Suddenly, her life yawned before her like a gaping dark hole. Without the things she'd anchored herself to, where would she go, who would she be?

Everything she'd done until now had a purpose. She'd had a brief to follow. She'd been needed. But when all this business with William Tanner and Cameron Enterprises was over, where would that leave her? She knew for herself, from the celebrity gossip magazines and articles, that men like him changed their mistresses as often as they changed their designer shirts. Even in the past week she'd seen conjecture in the *Seaside Gazette's* gossip column about who William Tanner would adorn his arm with next. The photos they'd shown of him with various other girlfriends, some of them supermodels, just made her heart ache even more.

Given what he was used to, was it even worth hoping that he could fall in love with someone like her—as she'd fallen in love with him?

Eight

Will sat at his desk in his office and leaned back in his chair. Tired and irritable after a difficult night, he'd given up on trying to sleep and had come into the office early. A lack of sleep was one thing. Something he was used to on occasion and something that he usually took in stride. The cause of last night's lack of sleep was quite another.

Margaret Cole had gotten to him.

Somehow she'd inveigled her way under his thick skin and settled like a burr. Now that he'd had her, he wanted more of her. He'd never felt a need such as that which now consumed him. He tried to rationalize it—to put it down to the exceptionally long period of time he'd waited from their first meeting back in February, to actually being able to be with her. Anticipation had a way of sweetening things, of increasing the expectations and pleasures to be discovered.

Yet, now that he'd been intimate with Margaret, rather than be assuaged, the anticipation had only built to greater heights.

Their intense physical connection had come as quite a surprise to him. A welcome one, nonetheless. There was no denying they lit up the sheets together. Margaret was an unexpectedly passionate and generous lover. Her lush feminine curves drove him crazy—whether she was clothed, or not.

Completely without guile or artifice, she'd simply been herself. That was a refreshing breath of air in a life that had become increasingly superficial in recent years. Or at least that was how he'd aimed to keep his relationships to the fairer sex. Light and commitment-free.

Which brought him to the question—could anyone really be that giving without an ulterior motive? His dealings with people in recent years would suggest not. Not even his father was above a bit of manipulation to get what he wanted. So where did that leave Will with Margaret?

He'd coerced her into their arrangement, a fact that hadn't bothered him in the least when he'd done it. But now, he wanted her to be with him because she wanted to be there. Not out of any misplaced loyalty to her younger sibling. Was she the kind of woman who would go so far as to sleep with a man to keep her brother out of jail? He'd told her she had to be convincing in her role as his fiancée. Did that extend to convincing him, too? If so, she was a damn good actress.

Any other man would probably tell him to simply accept his good fortune. Not only did he have someone prepared to act as his fiancée—without the usual pressure to make the situation genuine, to soothe his parents' ruffled feathers—at the same time she was willingly warming his sheets.

He was getting exactly what he wanted—more, even—and yet he still wasn't satisfied. Deep inside of him guilt festered over having forced Margaret's hand in this. Would she have come to him without the coercion of protecting Jason? He'd never know.

It was beginning to give him a headache. No matter

which way he looked at things, he kept coming back to the same point. She was fiercely loyal. A quality he held in the highest respect. Yet he'd used that loyalty against her and that knowledge left a bitter taste in his mouth.

William sighed deeply and shook his head. He knew, deep down, that he wasn't man enough to willingly let Margaret go. Now that he'd had a taste of her, there was no way he'd be so stupid as to give all that up. And, he reconciled himself, it wasn't as if she was getting nothing from their liaison. She carried herself with a newfound confidence since her makeover. He'd given her that. He'd allowed her to discover the real woman she was capable of being.

But no matter how much he tried to convince himself that the end justified the means, his attempts lay shallow on his conscience.

His cell phone chirped discreetly in his pocket and he reached for it, sliding it open without checking the caller ID—a fact he regretted the minute he heard his mother's voice on the other end.

"William? Would you care to explain how you came to be engaged and yet you neglected to tell your family of this event?"

"Mum, great to hear from you. How's Dad doing, and you, of course?"

"Don't think you can hedge with me, young man."

"I haven't been a young man for some years now." William smiled at his mother's tone. No matter how old he was, she still spoke to him as if he'd just come in from the garden with muddied clothes and all manner of scrapes and bumps on his body. "And my engagement is still new to me, by the way. I haven't had a chance to share the news with you before now. How did you hear about it, anyway?"

His mother mentioned the name of one of the tabloids she perused over her morning coffee each day. The news painted a grim smile on his face. So, the reporter who'd caught them coming out of the theater on Friday evening had followed them to the restaurant and seen Will give Margaret her ring. His story had obviously sold to a syndicated outlet. The news would be nationwide by now. It was what he'd wanted, wasn't it? And yet, there was a side of him that wished he could have kept it quiet just a little longer. Spared Margaret some of the notoriety that would be associated with their "engagement."

"Wow, that didn't take long."

"No matter how long it took, William, your father and I are disappointed you didn't see fit to include us in your news. I would have thought that given the circumstances we would have been the first to know."

Olivia Tanner's displeasure radiated through the phone lines from her New York brownstone, making William feel as if he was about eight years old all over again. Except her underlying threat now was far, far more powerful than any threat of withdrawal of privileges when he was a child.

"If the rug hadn't been pulled out from under me by the tabloid, you would have been receiving my call in the next few hours," he said smoothly. "Would it help any if I bring Margaret home to meet you and Dad at the end of this week?"

"This week? You can come that soon? Of course we'd love to meet her."

The sudden change in his mother's tone of voice should have made him laugh out loud, but he knew that her concern came from her deep-seated love for all her children.

"Sure, I have some business that's come up in New Jersey and I need to make the trip anyway. There's no reason why Margaret can't accompany me. Why don't you organize one of your famous dinners for Saturday night and invite the whole family over?"

"I hope everyone will be free at such short notice," she

mused out loud. "Never mind, I'll make sure it happens. Pre-dinner drinks at seven, then."

"Sounds good to me," Will agreed.

"Will you be staying in your apartment or would you like me to make up the guest room at home?"

Will's lips curled in a sardonic smile. Oh, he'd give his mother points for trying but she wasn't going to get her claws into Margaret that easily.

"I thought we'd stay in a hotel this time around. It's only a short visit. Hardly worth putting anyone out over it."

Despite the fact the concierge of his apartment building would happily see to stocking his refrigerator for a quick weekend visit home, Will didn't like the idea of taking Margaret there to stay. He'd had other women there and, for some reason, the very thought of associating Margaret with those others sat uncomfortably with him.

"So what's she like, this Margaret? I have to say I'm surprised at the speed with which you two have become engaged. I didn't even know you were seeing anyone."

Will chose his words carefully. "She's not like anyone I've ever dated before, that's for certain."

"Well, that's a relief. Those other girls were very shallow, Will. It was clear to both your father and me that you had no intention of settling down with any one of them. What drew you to this girl?"

"I couldn't help myself." He gave a rueful laugh. "I know it sounds clichéd, but I saw her across a crowded room and I just…"

Will's voice trailed off as he recalled what it had been like to see Margaret for the very first time. Even with her upper face masked, she'd caught his eye with her poise and the hints of beauty he saw beneath the costume she'd worn. It hit him again, square in the solar plexus—that sense of shock and yearning. The need to take, to possess. That need hadn't lessened. If anything, it had only grown stronger.

His mother's voice had softened considerably when she spoke again. "I can't wait to meet her, Will. She looks lovely in the picture in the paper."

"You'll like her even more in person."

"Well, you should let me go so I can start organizing things for Saturday. You haven't left me much time."

"Mum," he warned. "Just family for Saturday night. I don't want you to scare her off."

"Oh, of course I won't do any such thing. How could you even suggest it?"

He heard the humor behind Olivia Tanner's words and felt his lips tug into an answering smile.

"Gee, I really don't know. Maybe past experience?"

"Really, I have no idea what you're talking about. Now look at the time, I must go. Take care, Will. I love you, son."

"Love you, too, Mum. See you Saturday."

He disconnected the call with a wistful smile on his face. They really only wanted the best for him, he knew that. But it was endlessly frustrating to be continually treated like an infant. And therein lay the crux of most of his conflict with his parents. Being their youngest child, he supposed they'd found it harder to let go of him than his older brothers. A fact which had only made him rebel harder and push more firmly to be independent from a very young age. Even when his father had been offered a position with one of New York's leading financial institutions, and the family had transferred to the United States from their home in New Zealand, Will had insisted on remaining behind to finish his degree in accounting and finance at the University of Auckland.

As much as he loved his family, that time alone, without their well-meaning interference, had been a Godsend for him. And it had helped him make decisions about himself and the kind of future he wanted—one not unduly influenced by his parents' dreams for him or his older brothers' accomplishments. Decisions that had led him to work for Rafe Cameron and had ultimately led him here.

He was happy with his life, satisfied with where he'd worked his way. The work here in Vista del Mar, checking into the financial complexities of Rafe's latest acquisition, was the kind of challenge he loved to get his teeth into. And as for Margaret Cole, well, she was an enjoyable segue into the next stage of his life. A transitional relationship that was bringing him surprising delight and would ultimately bring him exactly what he wanted from his father.

"We're going to New York?" Margaret asked, surprise pitching her voice high.

"Yes, is that a problem?"

"To meet your family?" She paled and plunked herself down hard in the seat opposite Will's desk.

"It was always in the cards that they'd want to meet you when our relationship went into the public domain."

Margaret swallowed against the lump of fear in her throat. It was one thing pretending their engagement was real to her work colleagues, friends and Jason, but quite another to do so in front of his parents.

"But they know you. Surely they'll see right through us. What if I mess up?"

"Not if you keep on doing the stellar job you've been doing."

Will rose from his chair and walked around his desk. He bent and tipped Margaret's face up to his, giving her a short hard kiss that sent her scrambled senses totally haywire.

"Don't worry. You'll be fine. Just be you."

Just be you, he said. But the person Will Tanner knew was

not the person she'd been for so very long. The fight with Jason last night had been proof of that.

"Margaret?"

She blinked and realized he'd been talking to her. "Sorry, what did you say?"

"You can do this, you know. All you have to do is smile, be friendly and convince my parents you love me."

Margaret's stomach clenched into a painfully tight knot of tension. *Convince his parents she loved him?* After last night's torturous admission to herself that she was totally and utterly in love with him she'd hoped that she could somehow keep that monumental truth to herself. It would go at least some way toward protecting her when he walked away and returned to his life in New York and she was left here to pick up the pieces of her own.

Pretending she loved him would be the least of her worries this weekend. Of a far more pressing concern was what she'd do if he realized the truth of her emotional state.

Firming her resolve, Margaret gave a short nod.

"Of course I can do this. After all, you're paying me well to do the job you hired me to do. You can count on me."

The words were like ashes in her mouth but they gave her strength at the same time.

"They're not ogres, you know, my parents," Will said with a wry look on his face. "There's no need to be frightened. I will be with you."

"I know. It just kind of threw me. We've been so busy here that I hadn't stopped to think about meeting your family, especially with them all the way in New York."

"The opportunity presented itself. I thought it better to make the most of it. Have you been to New York before?"

"Never. Seriously, I haven't been anywhere farther than Anaheim when I was a kid to visit Disneyland."

Fleetingly, Margaret thought of the map she'd destroyed

in her bedroom last night. New York had been one of her markers. One of the first she'd carefully placed when travel had been one of her big dreams. Well, if she had nothing else after all this, she'd at least have this journey to look back on.

"We'll have to make it worthwhile for you, then," Will said decisively. "I'll show you around."

"I'd like that," she said with a smile, making a solid decision to grasp every minute of the unexpected bonus of the trip to New York.

The next couple of days at work went quickly for Margaret. Will spent a great deal of time in meetings with Rafe Cameron—meetings that extended into the evenings, leaving her to her own devices. She was puzzled when those meetings didn't generate a great deal of work coming back her way. She would have thought that she'd be hard at work typing up summaries, projections and reports as a result, but maybe this was a temporary lull. She took advantage of the respite to ensure all her work was completely up-to-date so she could head away knowing she was coming back to a clear desk.

As he had with their foray into San Diego, Will had taken care of all their arrangements for the visit to New York. He'd suggested they leave early on Friday morning. With the time differences between the West and East coasts they'd be arriving at JFK in the late afternoon. Time, hopefully, to see a little of the city before sunset.

Will picked her up from her home before sunrise and Margaret felt an air of excitement as she wheeled her case out and locked the front door behind her. She would be traveling on a plane for the first time in her life and, despite the obscenely early hour, she felt as energized as a sugar addict locked in a candy shop.

"Got everything you need?" Will asked as he met her at the door and took her case from her.

"I think so," she said.

"There's something you've forgotten."

"No, I think I have everything," Margaret said, mentally running through her list of things she'd packed.

"This," Will said succinctly as he bent to kiss her.

As ever, Margaret's entire body rushed to aching, pulsing life. He tasted of a pleasant combination of mint and fresh coffee and she kissed him back with all the fervor and abandon she'd been holding back since their weekend in San Diego. She'd missed seeing him, being with him in every sense of the word, and their all too brief times together in the office had only sharpened her hunger for him—for this.

Will broke free with a groan and rested his forehead against hers. His breathing was uneven, his heart pounding in his chest beneath the flat of her hand.

"I think I should have requested the company jet for this trip. At least then we might have had a little privacy on the flight," he said, his breathing now slowly returning to normal.

"I missed you this week," she answered simply.

"I'll make it up to you, I promise," he said and gave her another quick kiss before lifting her bag and carrying it to the waiting car in the driveway.

The driver alighted from the car as they approached and stowed her case in the trunk while Will held the door open for her. She slid into her seat and he moved in alongside her. In the climate-controlled interior of the car she welcomed the warmth of his body against hers but she held her posture straight and erect. As much as she wished she could snuggle into his side, she wasn't sure enough of her position with him to do so. Even after last weekend, while they'd conquered some of the physical distance between them in their make-believe relationship, she still didn't feel comfortable breaching the invisible boundaries he had erected between them.

Traffic had yet to build up on the freeway and the trip to the San Diego airport went smoothly, as did check-in. Margaret's eyes widened in surprise as they were greeted by name by the cabin crew and shown to their seats in first class. Will ushered her into the window seat before stowing his briefcase in the overhead compartment.

As he settled into his seat beside her, she turned to look at him.

"First class?" she hissed under her breath.

"Why not?" he replied smoothly. "It's your first flight, isn't it? May as well be memorable."

Margaret shook her head in wonder as she looked again at the man who'd given her so much in such a short period of time. He would never understand how much this meant to her. For him, traveling this way was commonplace. But for her, it was something she'd never have achieved in her wildest dreams. She sat back and gazed out the side window, a sudden glaze of tears hazing her vision.

What would he be like with the woman he loved? she wondered. He'd give her the world on a gilded platter. Whoever she was, she would be the luckiest woman on the planet. How Margaret wished it could be her.

Nine

A discreetly uniformed driver stood with a card bearing William's name as they exited the baggage claim area at JFK. Before Margaret realized it, they were being shown into a shining limousine and the car was pulling into traffic leading onto the Van Wyck Expressway.

Will was an excellent guide, noting points of interest as they drove along the expressway. All in all, the trip only took about half an hour and Margaret was totally enchanted as they pulled up outside their stately looking hotel on East 55th Street.

As Will helped her from the car she said, "You have a thing for classic architecture, don't you? First the hotel in San Diego, and now this?"

"Blame it on my good old Kiwi upbringing." He smiled in return. "My parents were very much into ensuring we had the necessities as kids, but not luxuries, at least not until we were older and could be relied upon not to break anything. Staying in places like this is one of my indulgences."

"But don't you have a home here in New York?"

"An apartment, yes, but since we're only here for a few nights I didn't see the point in having it aired and stocked with perishables when we could stay here."

Margaret nodded. She could see the point in that, but she was curious to see what his residence was like. He let so little of himself out in the course of a day at work, exhibiting only the kind of concentrated control that had sent his reputation ahead of him during the Worth Industries takeover.

Even in bed she'd felt as if he held something back. Not completely surprising, she supposed, when their attraction, on his part at least, was purely physical.

She was distracted from her thoughts as they checked into the hotel and were shown to their suite. Named for one of the original owners of the hotel, the suite was plushly appointed and Margaret could barely stop oohing and ahhing over the furnishings and accoutrements. Will watched her with an indulgent look on his face that made her feel quite naive and inexperienced but, when she thought about it, it would be a sad day for her when such delights became commonplace. As if that was likely to ever happen, she reminded herself as she checked her reflection in the mirror of the opulent marble bathroom. No, she had to make the most of every second of this. Every second with him.

Once she'd freshened up, she and Will rode the elevator back down to the street. There were people everywhere, it seemed—office workers at the end of their day, tourists looking about with the same wide-eyed wonder Margaret knew was on her face.

"How's your head for heights?" Will asked as he pulled her hand through the crook of his elbow and led her around the corner and onto 5th Avenue.

"I'm okay, why?"

"I thought we'd start your introduction to New York with an overview of the city, from the Empire State Building."

"Seriously? Is it like they show in the movies?"

"Depends on the movie, I suppose, but yeah. Come on and I'll show you. What would you prefer, walk or cab?"

"Oh, walk, please."

"Walk it is, then."

Margaret was surprised that it took them less than half an hour to reach their destination. All along 5th Avenue her attention had been captured by the amazing storefronts and buildings. After they'd gone through security screening, Will bought their tickets and they followed a group of people to the elevators that would take them up to the 80th floor. Margaret had to hold on to her stomach as the elevator car traveled upward.

"Wow," she laughed, a little shakily. "That makes the elevators at work seem positively snail-like."

"There's one more ride up, to the 86th floor. Unless you'd rather take the stairs?"

"No, I'll be fine."

Will smiled back and took her hand as they joined the queue waiting to be shown into the cars that would take them up the tower to the observatory level.

"Oh, my," she breathed as she and Will left the car and walked out into the viewing area. "I knew it would be something else, but this...this really is something else." As far as she could see, the city stretched out like a three-dimensional patchwork of color, texture and light interspersed by water and bridges. "It's so huge."

"Never fails to take my breath away," Will commented as he stood close behind her, wrapping his arms around her waist.

The warmth of his body against her back was most welcome, almost grounding for her. Just feeling him there behind her gave her a sense of security. Even though they were surrounded by other tourists, all clamoring and pointing as they took in the cityscape spread before them, they could have been completely alone. She leaned back against his solid strength, relishing the moment and tucking it away in a corner of her mind. This experience was something she would never forget in all her days.

In the end, they spent nearly an hour on the viewing deck, looking at the city from all aspects. She'd shuddered as they looked below at the streets teeming with traffic. From up on the observation deck it didn't seem real, it was as if what happened beneath them was another world completely, one devoid of sound, yet she knew it was completely the opposite.

The sun had begun to set, casting long shadows over the city. Will teased her about wanting to stay until full dark so she could see the city lights spread out like a pirate's sparkling treasure chest, but the long shadow of the Empire State Building stretching out like a dark finger over the buildings beneath them reminded her that their time together was fleeting and there was still so very much she wanted to experience with Will in his adopted home city.

Will found Margaret's open enjoyment in New York utterly refreshing. Aside from one moment, shortly before they left the observation deck of the Empire State Building, where she'd suddenly appeared pensive and quiet, she'd displayed an unabashed joy in everything she experienced. Even now she clutched a souvenir pewter replica of the building in her hand, pointing out where they'd stood and watched the city bustle beneath them.

Seeing her like this, so different from the cool composed assistant who worked for him in the office, made him realize just how far he'd pushed her out of her comfort zone with this trip, and it made him want to see more of this side of her. He wanted to be the one to show her more of everything—starting with New York and leading who knew where.

He wondered what she'd think of his parents' place in Manhattan. His mother was inordinately proud of the brownstone where they lived. She'd always loved being in a busy city, even back home in New Zealand. Suburbia had never really been her thing, but she'd tolerated it so he and his brothers could have a big backyard to play in. Once his brothers had graduated high school, and while he was still attending, they'd moved into a luxury apartment building in Auckland. The eventual move to New York had seen his mother find her spiritual home and she hadn't been homesick, ever.

Beneath his arm he felt Margaret shiver a little. The evening temperature had dropped, reminding him that while he was quite used to New York's climate, his West Coast companion was not. The coat she wore did little to cut the chill, so he hailed a cab to take them to their next destination. If she enjoyed the Empire State Building so much, he had no doubt she'd enjoy what he had planned next.

Times Square at night had to be seen to be believed, and if the look of awe on Margaret's face was any indicator, she was having trouble believing anything anymore.

"What on earth do they do in a power outage?" she asked as she looked from one brilliant display to the next.

Will just shrugged before changing the subject. "Hungry? I know your body clock is probably still on California time, but we missed lunch somewhere along the way and I'm starving."

"Sure, but nothing fancy, okay?" she insisted.

He knew just the place that would appeal to her. The intimately lit Greek restaurant he frequented in the theater district was the perfect solution to both her tourist instinct and the grumbling hole in his belly. It was inexpensive and casual, and he knew she'd enjoy its atmosphere, not to mention the highly-rated food. But by the time they'd been seated and enjoyed their entrées he could see she was beginning to droop.

"Don't tell me you're getting tired already?" he cajoled.

"It's all just so much to take in today. So many firsts. Really, you have no idea."

No, he didn't. There was so much about Margaret he didn't know and so much she didn't know about him, either. Things that might be necessary for them to carry off the dinner at his parents' tomorrow night. The reminder was sobering.

"Are you up to a little conversation?" he coaxed.

"Sure, what did you want to talk about?"

"Tomorrow evening."

"Oh, yes. That." She shifted uncomfortably in her chair. "I know you said I should just be 'me.' But do you honestly think I'll be okay? I'm sure I'm nothing like your other wo—"

"You'll be fine," he interrupted, not wanting to even think about other women when he was with her. "It won't be any different than at work. If we stick as close to the truth as possible—meeting at the ball in February, keeping things quiet but that our feelings just overtook us—then they'll take it hook, line and sinker. Dad might work in finance but he's an incurable romantic. He'll be only too happy just to see me engaged."

"What about your past? You know, school, hobbies, things I should probably know about you."

"Given that we haven't known each other that long, I think they'll be satisfied with what you already know about me. After all, we supposedly have the rest of our lives to get to know one another's secrets."

Margaret turned her glass on its coaster, a small frown

on her face. "Doesn't it bother you at all, that we're lying to them?"

Will stiffened. "It bothers me that I have to," he said coldly.

Margaret reached out a hand and placed it on his thigh under their table. "I'm sorry. I didn't mean to make you mad."

He placed his hand over hers before speaking. "I'm not mad at you. Just angry with the situation. You're helping me here, and I appreciate it." He sighed—the sound a short huff of air. "Look, I know we didn't exactly embark on this in the most friendly or pleasant way, but you're not unhappy, are you?"

"No, I'm fine. Really. I appreciate that you gave Jason a second chance. I'm just sorry it had to come to that. But as to how things have developed with us, well, I'd prefer to think that's something separate from what brought us together." She looked sad for a moment, but then she flicked her gaze up to his—her dark brown eyes glowing warm in her face. "Can we head back to the hotel now?"

Will felt an answering heat spread through his body as he interpreted the look in her eyes. They could continue their talk later. Much later.

In the short cab ride back to their hotel Margaret struggled with her thoughts. All day, Will had been attentive and kind, and she'd allowed herself to once again sink into the fantasy that they were a couple—a real couple. She needed to retrain herself. To stop hoping for what couldn't be. Talking with him about tomorrow night had forced her to take a reality check. She might not be able to be with him the way she wanted, but she'd take what she could get.

Will tossed the key card onto the side table in the entrance to their suite and closed the door behind her.

"Would you like a drink?" he asked, crossing to the mini-bar.

"No, actually. There's only one thing I really want right now."

She closed the distance between them, shrugging off her coat along the way and letting it drop on one of the chairs in the sitting room.

Will smiled at her, a smile that did funny things to her insides and heightened the tightly coiled tension in the pit of her belly.

"Is that right?" he asked, his voice suddenly thick with desire.

"Oh, yes, and I think I know just the man who will give it to me," she teased as she ran her hands up over his chest.

Beneath the thickness of his sweater she could feel the lean muscle she knew corded his body. She skimmed her hands up to his shoulders before linking her fingers at the back of his head and drawing his face down to hers. Her boldness surprised her, all along in their orchestrated union she'd been the one acted upon. Now it was her turn to take control.

She traced the outline of his lips with the tip of her tongue before pressing her lips to his. His arms banded tight around her, drawing her against his strength, letting her know in no uncertain terms that he wanted her. The knowledge gave her license to do what she wanted and it was a power she relished.

Her entire body vibrated with need for him and she could barely wait to be skin to skin. Reluctantly breaking their embrace, she took his hand and led him to the bedroom where she pushed him, none too gently, onto the luxurious covers. She followed him into the enveloping softness and kissed him again, this time sucking his lower lip into her mouth and laving it with her tongue. He groaned into her mouth, his hands shoving aside her blouse and caressing her back before he skimmed his hands down to palm her buttocks and press her lower body tight against his.

An electric current of sensation shot from her core as she flexed against him, against the hard ridge of his desire for her. Eager to repeat the sensation, Margaret let her legs fall to either side of his and pushed herself upright, leaving only the apex of her thighs connecting with his groin. She looked down at him and smiled.

Will gripped her hips and tilted her against him and she flexed again.

"You're killing me here," he growled.

"I know, isn't it great?" she teased.

Her fingers flew to the buttons of her blouse and one by one she slid them free, before shrugging the garment off her shoulders. She was wearing one of her new bras, one she'd chosen herself with a boldness she'd never indulged in before. She'd never been comfortable with her body, but when she'd tried this bra on she'd felt incredible. The café au lait-colored lace, appliquéd over black satin, appealed to a decadent side of her she'd never really known existed, and the cut was something else—exposing the soft globes of her breasts while barely concealing her nipples.

"Do you like it?" she asked.

Will trailed his fingers across the smooth rounds, his touch sending tiny shocks sizzling through her. When he traced the outside edge of the scalloped lace, his fingertip almost brushed against her nipple and she shivered in delight.

"I like it very much," Will said, his voice a low rumble. "But I like what's inside it more."

Before she could stop him, his hand snaked around to her back and he'd flicked open the clasps. He pulled the confection of satin and lace away from her, exposing her to his ravenous gaze.

"Yes, that's much better," he said.

Will jackknifed up from beneath her, cupping her breasts in his hands and burying his face in their fullness. She felt the heat of his breath against her skin and let her head drop back, arching her back so nothing restricted him. He traced the outline of one nipple with his tongue, while gently squeezing the other between one finger and a thumb. Sensation spiraled through her, increasing in intensity as it arrowed to her center. Gone were all feelings of self-consciousness or embarrassment about her body. Instead, all she felt was the overwhelming sense that this was so very right.

And she wanted more of it.

Somehow, through the sensual assault on her senses, she found the capability to reach for the bottom edge of Will's sweater and began to tug it up over his torso. He reluctantly relinquished her to help her denude him of both his sweater and the shirt he'd worn beneath it. She felt him shudder as she lightly scratched her fingernails across his shoulders and down over his chest.

He pulled her to him and Margaret gasped at the warm shock of his skin against hers. At the delicious pressure of his chest against her breasts. He nipped lightly at the sensitive skin of her neck and she clutched his upper arms in response, her nails digging into him as a sharp, involuntary pull from deep inside her swelled and threatened to consume her.

Will peppered her neck and shoulders with fleeting kisses, his hands once again at her breasts. She loved the feel of his strong fingers on her body, loved the way he made her feel.

Loved him.

She might never be able to tell him the truth of her feelings, she realized, but she could show him with every caress, every gesture, exactly how much he meant to her. She put her hands to his shoulders and pushed him backward, tumbling forward onto him as he allowed himself to drop back onto the bed again. Her lips found his and meshed with them, tongues dueling in a sacred dance of mutual worship.

She forced herself to break the kiss, to drag herself upright and to reach for his belt and the fastenings on his jeans. His fingers tangled with hers.

"No, let me," she bid softly.

His eyes clouded and became heavy-lidded as she undid his jeans, exposing his boxer briefs and the prominent erection that strained against the stretched cotton. She stroked him through the fabric and felt him strain against her fingers. With as much grace as she could muster, she slipped off the bed to her feet and dragged off his boots and socks, then pulled his jeans down and off his long legs before easing his briefs away from his body and tossing them behind her.

He was magnificent. For a moment she just drank in the sight of him lying there on the bed. Hers for the taking. But then need overtook her and she quickly kicked off her shoes and yanked off her socks before shimmying out of her trousers and panties.

Even though it had been only a week since his eyes had feasted upon her naked form, the sheer beauty of her took his breath away again. From the fall of glossy black hair to her creamy shoulders, to the mouthwatering fullness of her breasts. From the smallness of her waist to the very feminine flair of her hips. She was all woman—every delectable inch of her. Would it be like this every time they made love? he wondered fleetingly. This awe and amazement in the perfection of her body?

He sucked in a breath as she straddled his legs—the smooth skin of her inner thighs like silk against him. The heat of her core, calling to him. When her fingers closed around his aching shaft he caught hold of the bedcovers, his hands twisting in the finely woven fabric as tight as they could in an effort to resist the urge to thrust within the gentle sheath of her fist.

She was driving him out of his mind with her touch and as she bent forward, her hair drifted over him, as gossamer soft and fine as a breath. He could have lost it right there and then, her effect upon him was so intense. But instant gratification had never been his thing. No, far, far better to prolong the ecstasy. To draw pleasure out for as long as humanly possible before giving in to the inevitable.

Will had cause to question his resolve as in the next breath he felt her lush mouth close over his tip. Felt the swirl of her tongue over the ultra-sensitive surface. Again and again. She took him deeper in the heated cavern of her mouth, her hand working firmly on his shaft and he knew without a shadow of a doubt that he'd lost all semblance of being in charge of himself. He'd never submitted as completely as this to anyone. He'd always held back a level of control, choosing when he'd let go. But this was completely different. Margaret held his pleasure in her power. It was thrilling and daunting at the same time.

As she increased the pressure of her hand and her mouth, he felt his climax build inside him, out of control, banishing thought and replacing it with the sure knowledge that what would come next would be bigger, brighter and better than anything he'd ever known before. Every nerve in his body was poised for the intensity of the pleasure escalating through his body. Pleasure she gave him.

And then it burst through him, pulse after pulse of rapture, each one stronger than the one before. A raw cry of completion ripped from his throat as bliss invaded his every cell, suffusing him with a boneless sense of well-being. He reached for Margaret and drew her into his arms, her body aligning with his, her hair a swath of black-velvet softness across his chest and shoulders.

Words couldn't adequately describe how she'd made him feel or the depth of his confusion when it related to her. Outside of the bedroom she was Miss Prim. Carrying herself with poise and an air of quiet efficiency, as if she moved in a sea of calm. Yet, in the bedroom she was something else altogether. And that lingerie. He was tempted to ask her to put it back on, just so he could peel it off her all over again.

He stroked a hand down her long smooth spine, over the curve of her rounded buttocks. Despite the intensity of his climax, he could feel his body begin to stir to life again, and this time he relished the fact that he'd be the one bringing her pleasure.

He rolled them both onto their sides and continued his slow lazy exploration of her body.

"You have the softest skin," he murmured. "Makes me want to kiss you all over."

"So what's stopping you?" she answered, a slow smile curving her mouth.

"Absolutely nothing," he answered and leaned forward to capture that smile with his lips before he nuzzled her neck, inhaling the sweet, intoxicating scent of her skin.

Nothing else in the world came close to it, he decided. Once you got past the "touch me not" signals that she sent out, you discovered the many layers that made her who she was and the treats she had in store for a man like him. A man who was prepared to bring her the world of delight. Who could worship her as she deserved to be worshipped.

He traced the cord of her neck with his tongue, smiling to himself as she let out a soft moan, and committing the erogenous zone to memory. Next he followed the line of her collarbone, from just below her shoulder until he found the hollow at the base of her throat. A tiny kiss there to punctuate his journey and he continued across her collarbone to the other side. Beneath him, Margaret squirmed and pressed her shoulders back hard into the bedcovers, thrusting her breasts proudly forward. Never a man to waste an opportunity, Will trailed his tongue over one creamy swell—working in an ever-decreasing spiral that led to her tightly budded nipple.

Her breath came in shallow gasps as he drew closer to his ultimate goal, and halted for several excruciatingly long seconds as his mouth hovered over the distended tip.

"Please?" she begged, her voice no more than a tortured whisper.

"Your wish is my command," he answered.

He blew a cool breath over the taut bead, then outlined it carefully with the firm tip of his tongue. She arched even more, thrusting upward in complete supplication and he finally gave her what she wanted. He closed his lips around her, drawing the peak into his mouth and suckling hard.

She cried out his name, her fingers suddenly tunneling through his hair and holding his head to her. Her extreme sensitivity drove his body to even greater demands but he held himself in check. This time, it was all about her.

He eased off the pressure of his tongue, his lips, then built them once more before transferring his attention to her other breast. Again he followed the painstaking path of the decreasing spiral. Again he felt her body grow taut, her back arch, until he at last gave in and lavished his mouth upon her.

She was on the edge of orgasm, he realized with a sense of wonder. Purely from his ministrations to her nipples. He'd heard of it, but never before experienced it with a lover. Her very responsiveness and abandon made his control stretch tight, but he renewed his attention to her, his hands gently molding the shape of her breasts with a reverence he'd never experienced before.

Her release, when it came, sent her entire body rigid, before she collapsed back onto the bed. Will rested his head a moment on her breasts, feeling her rapid breathing as it slowly returned to normal.

"I've never done that before," she said from beneath him, her voice filled with wonder.

Her hands came to rest on his shoulders, her fingertips drawing tiny circles on his skin. Even the lightest touch from her drove him crazy. He shifted, pulling himself higher over her body so they were face to face. Her hands coasted down his back, past his waist to his buttocks. The feather-light touch had him totally wired on top of having just brought her to orgasm.

"You okay with it?" he asked.

She seemed to think about it for a few seconds before a beatific smile spread across her face. "Oh, yes. Most definitely."

"Good, then let's not stop there."

Will reached for the box of condoms he'd shoved under his pillow before they went sightseeing and ripped it open, scattering the foil packets on the covers beside them.

"So many?" Margaret commented.

"So few," he laughed in return.

He grabbed one of the condoms and ripped away the foil before sheathing himself and returning to the warmth of Margaret's embrace. Positioning himself with his knees spread wide on the bed, he dragged her hips toward him, and pulled her legs over his thighs.

His blunt head probed at the moist entrance to her body. He tore his gaze away from the compelling view of their bodies joining together and watched her face instead as he eased his length inside her. Her inner muscles clenched tight around him, and he hesitated a moment, allowing her to ease and accept him. The control he had to employ made sweat break out on his back. A trickle of moisture ran down his spine to the cleft of his buttocks, the sensation it evoked driving his hips forward until he was buried within her.

A flush of color spread over her chest and she moved beneath him, silently encouraging him to continue. Her lips parted on an indrawn breath as he withdrew then drove into her again slowly.

"More," she whispered. "Don't stop."

Determined to give her pleasure before he lost all semblance of command, he began to thrust deep within her—at first slow and then with increasing pressure until he felt as if he was going to shatter. Margaret's hands gripped his forearms, her fingernails digging into his skin as he increased momentum, her breath coming in short, sharp cries of pleasure until her entire body spasmed and she let go with a gut-deep groan of satisfaction. The sound of her, the feel of her, the pulsating strength of her orgasm, drove him over the edge and beyond. His hips jerked against her as ecstasy flooded through him and he gave himself over to the sensation.

Over to her.

Ten

They were on the ferry coming back from the Statue of Liberty and Margaret still felt as if she was lost in the haze of the rapture they'd explored together. If Will had suggested they forego her continued introduction to his home city and stay in their suite for the rest of the day she would have happily agreed.

Sleep had been snatched in small increments during the night and through part of this morning, and in between they'd indulged in one another virtually every way she could have imagined. She would have thought that her desire for him would have diminished, but she only wanted him more. Even now, tucked against his side, his arm around her shoulders, her body hummed with suppressed energy. Energy she knew exactly how to expend.

Her wonder in the incredible monument she'd just visited paled in comparison to the wonder she felt every time he touched her. Whether it was as intimate as his caress across her clitoris as a precursor to bringing her to yet another amazing peak of pleasure, or whether it was something as simple as brushing a strand of hair from her cheek, when Will touched her she was instantly and irrevocably on fire for him.

Will bent his head and pressed a kiss against her temple. "Enjoying today?"

"Very much," she said with a smile.

"I have something else planned for you."

"Oh, something that involves you, too, I hope."

"Later tonight, yes. But when we get back to the hotel I need to leave you for a couple of hours."

"Could I come with you?" Margaret asked, sensing his response in the way he pulled away from her.

"Not this time. It's just some business. It shouldn't take more than a couple of hours."

"Business? On a Saturday."

"It can't be avoided."

She studied his face. It was as if he'd become someone else. The corporate Will Tanner, not the lover who'd painstakingly brought her to a state of frenzy so many times last night.

"If it's business, why can't I come with you?" she pressed.

"Because of the special treat I've arranged for you. Besides, I don't want you to be bored and I do want you looking your best for tonight. Don't worry about anything except for being the perfect fiancée," he said, lifting her left hand to his mouth and pressing his lips to her ring finger.

By looking her best, he obviously meant looking polished within an inch of her life, she decided when he left her in the entrance of the beauty spa at the hotel with four hours to spare before they were due to leave for his parents' apartment. Did he not trust her to be able to present herself well to his family?

The thought tarnished the cloud of joy she'd been enveloped in for the past day and a half.

The irrefutable reminder that their entire relationship was a sham, despite their physical affinity, was a much needed wake-up call. She was playing a part and would do well to hold on to that truth. Already she risked far more hurt than she'd ever counted on by falling in love with him.

Well, if he wanted polished and perfect, that's exactly what he'd get. Margaret tried to tuck away her disappointment but it was easier said than done. By the time she'd been waxed, massaged, tinted and made up she felt even more tense, if that was possible.

Despite Will's assurances last night that they'd be able to carry off their elaborate web of deception in front of his family, she was feeling almost sick to her stomach. Even the exceptional glass of French champagne she'd been given during her pedicure failed to quell the nerves that held her muscles hostage.

What if his family hated her on sight? He'd be no nearer to a resolution to his quest. Worse, what if his family adored her? Would she and Will then be expected to maintain their deception even longer? Already her heart was fully engaged. She knew she wasn't going to be able to walk away from this, from him, without pain. But she knew without fail that staying with him for very much longer would be equally, if not more, damaging. And yet, even at her most pragmatic, she had to admit that there'd always be a part of her that clung to the distant hope that they could make this real. That the fairy tale could come true.

By the time Will rushed into their suite a bare ten minutes before they were due to leave, she still felt no more confident about her ability to carry this off tonight. While he grabbed a quick shower she set out the clothes he'd told her he wanted to wear. He came through from the en-suite bathroom, followed by a cloud of steam and the inimitable scent that she would forever associate with him.

As she sat on the bed and watched him finish getting ready it struck her as ironic that he'd given her four hours to prepare for tonight while only leaving himself ten minutes.

"What's so funny?" he asked, catching her eye in the mirror while he adjusted his tie.

"Oh, just that you seemed to think I needed so much time to be ready for tonight."

"Didn't you enjoy your time in the spa? I thought all women loved to be pampered."

"Oh, I enjoyed the pampering but I did start to wonder just how much work you thought I'd need."

He reached out and caught her arm, pulling her up to him. "You're really worried about that?"

"Not worried, exactly. Not about that, anyway."

"As far as I'm concerned, you don't need all that primping, ever. You're beautiful. I knew you were anxious about tonight and I thought it would be a nice relaxing way for you to spend the rest of the afternoon."

"I'd rather have been with you," Margaret said.

"You'd have been crazy with boredom. Believe me. Now," he flicked a look at his watch, "we'd better get going or my mother will skin me alive."

"You're afraid of your mother?" she asked, one perfectly shaped brow raised in disbelief.

"Let's just say I respect her and her expectation of punctuality."

Despite her nervousness, Margaret soon relaxed once she was behind the doors of the Tanners' brownstone in the Upper East Side. Will's mother, Olivia, refused to stand on ceremony and enveloped Margaret in a giant hug the moment she'd shed her coat.

"Welcome to the family, Margaret. We've all been dying to see you," Olivia said warmly. "Come through and meet everyone. Better to get it over with quickly, that way you can relax and just enjoy yourself for the rest of the evening."

Margaret instantly warmed to the older woman, who tucked a hand in the crook of Margaret's elbow and led her away from Will and through the immaculately furnished apartment to the main sitting room. Tastefully furnished in shades of green and cream, accented with black and white animal prints here and there, the room could have graced the cover of any of the glossy home magazines Margaret occasionally daydreamed over. The hardwood floors were polished to a mirror finish, yet still retained the well-used and homey feel of a home that was lived in and enjoyed, not just used as a showcase of wealth and position.

"This is Michael, he's Will's eldest brother, and this is his wife, Jane."

Margaret was immediately struck by the likeness between Michael and Will. It was in the eyes, and the intensity in their gaze. She felt as if she was being analyzed on multiple levels before he smiled and thrust out his hand.

"Call me Mike," he insisted, his fingers enveloping hers and shaking her hand.

"Mike, pleased to meet you." Margaret smiled back. She turned to the petite blonde at his side, "And, Jane, lovely to meet you, too."

"Welcome to the clan," Jane said with a quick smile. "Are you sure you know what you're letting yourself in for?"

"Not at all." Margaret laughed.

"Probably for the best," said another man who joined them. "I'm Paul. Middle son, best-looking and by far the most popular family member."

"Oh, you are not," interrupted the elegantly coiffed brunette who rose from the sofa where she'd been sitting.

As the woman's flowing outfit settled around her body, Margaret couldn't help but notice she was heavily pregnant. It drove home to her what a close unit this family was—and what an imposter she was.

The brunette sidled up next to her husband. "You'll have to excuse Paul's delusions of grandeur. I'm Kelly, and this," she patted her belly proudly, "will be Quin."

"Congratulations to you both," Margaret said, painting a smile on her face. "You must be very excited."

"Excited, scared, all the above," Kelly responded with a laugh.

"Who's this, then? Why haven't we been introduced yet?"

An older man, tall and lean and with gray receding hair and wire-rimmed glasses, materialized through an arched doorway.

"This is Margaret, Will's fiancée," Olivia said, drawing Margaret forward. "Margaret, this is Albert, Will's dad and, for his sins, my husband."

Despite her words, it was obvious there was a deep love and respect between the two.

"So this is the miracle woman who is going to take my boy down the aisle, hmm?"

Albert Tanner scrutinized Margaret from behind the lenses of his glasses. As with his eldest son, Mike, Margaret felt as if she were under a microscope but she held his gaze, not backing down for a second.

"I don't know about miracle woman," she said softly, "but yes, I'm Margaret Cole, and I'm pleased to meet you, Mr. Tanner."

The man's face wreathed in a wide smile. "Call me Al, we don't stand on ceremony here. Besides, if I'm to be your father-in-law, you can hardly spend the rest of your days calling me Mr. Tanner, now, can you? So, what can I get you to drink?"

Half an hour later, Margaret could feel herself begin to relax in increments. From across the room she saw Will, deep in conversation with Paul and Mike, while she sat talking to Jane and Kelly. Will chose that exact moment to look up, his eyes meeting hers. He gave her a small smile and lifted his glass toward her in a silent toast. The last vestiges of tension in her shoulders eased away. It was okay. She was doing okay.

When Olivia called everyone through to the dining room, Margaret was surprised when Albert came and took her arm.

"Since you're the guest of honor tonight, you get to sit near me," he said with a wink. "Besides, those women can't monopolize you all night. I want to get to know you better, too."

He seated Margaret to his right at the long table before taking his position at the head of the table. He was an amusing dinner companion, disclosing stories about Will when he was younger that brought the whole table roaring to laughter on several occasions. Will accepted the attention with good grace, however, he wasn't above sharing a few stories of his own about his brothers and his father.

It didn't take a rocket scientist to see the family was very close-knit. Even Jane and Kelly were an integral part of the special weave that drew them all together. Margaret continued to play her part, smiling and laughing along with the rest of them, but deep down inside she ached to belong.

Later, when they retired to the sitting room for coffee and liqueurs, Will made a point of sitting on the arm of the chair she settled in. His arm lay lightly across the back of her shoulders and she allowed herself to lean into him. She told herself it was just for show, she was merely keeping up her end of the bargain and helping him to achieve the goal he sought so avidly. But she knew she was grasping at straws. Happy to get what she could, while she could, because in a few more weeks this would no doubt be nothing more than a fond and distant memory.

By the time they left, it was well past midnight and there was a great deal of noise, hugs and promises to organize another night together as soon as Will and Margaret could get back to New York. Her ears were almost ringing with the friendly farewells as she and Will got into the back of the limousine he'd ordered.

In the darkened compartment she let her head drop back against the leather headrest and let go a deep sigh.

"Tired?" Will asked, his fingers lacing through hers.

"No, not exactly."

"You did brilliantly tonight. They adored you."

"Thank you. The feeling was mutual. Which is why it bothers me that…" Her voice trailed off into the shadows.

"Bothers you?" he prompted, giving her hand a gentle squeeze.

"That it was all such a lie."

"Don't worry, Margaret. By the time I tell them we've gone our separate ways we'll have achieved what we set out to do. As for Mum and Dad, well, they'll be disappointed but they'll get over it."

Sure they would, she thought. But would she? The question rattled through her mind over and over but she knew she was helpless to escape the truth of its answer. Instead, she sought surcease in the only thing she knew would distract her. The minute they set foot back in their suite, Margaret turned to Will and kissed him with the pent-up longing she'd been building all night long.

He didn't disappoint her—returning her passion with equal fervor, peeling away the layers of her clothing one by one until she was naked, all except for her hold-up stockings and her high-heeled pumps. They didn't even make it to the bedroom the first time. Instead, Will began to make love to her right there in the sitting room of their suite, paying homage to her breasts as only he could until her entire body quivered in anticipation. When he turned her around and placed her hands on the back of the large sofa that faced the main windows looking out onto 5th Avenue, she found herself clutching at the upholstery fabric as he positioned himself behind her.

She didn't have to wait long. A telltale sound of foil tearing, the slick of a condom onto his erection and he was there—the blunt head of his penis probing her wet folds, in, out. Only just so far and no farther. Teasing, driving her insane with wanting him. Wanting his possession of her.

His hands slid around her, to her belly, then up to her ribs until he cupped her breasts, his forefingers and thumbs squeezing her nipples. Sharp jolts of pleasure shot from the tips of her breasts to her core, making her inner muscles clench tight, then release. As if he knew how her body ached for him, he pushed himself deeper within her. Margaret shifted her feet slightly and tilted her hips forward. The knowledge that all he saw of her now was the length of her back and the roundness of her buttocks sent an illicit thrill through her body. A thrill that was rapidly eclipsed by the sensation of him thrusting within her, his hips cushioned by her backside as he drove himself deeper.

She braced her arms, meeting his thrusts with a need that threatened to overwhelm her. Close, she was so close. He squeezed her nipples again, simultaneously penetrating deep into her body, touching some magical spot within her that sent her screaming over the edge into a blinding orgasm. Will's sharp cry of satisfaction signaled his simultaneous release and he collapsed over her back, both their bodies now slippery with sweat.

Tremors still rocked her body. Diminishing aftershocks of pleasure that made her clench against him, holding him tight within the sheath of her body as if she never wanted to let him go. She moaned in protest as he began to withdraw from her and he pressed his lips to her back, just between her shoulder blades, sending a shiver down her spine.

"Let's take this into the bedroom," he whispered against her skin.

"I don't think I can move," she said, her voice still thick with the aftermath of their desire.

She heard Will laugh softly before he swept her into his arms, holding her tightly against him.

"Don't worry, I'll take care of you," he promised.

And, just like that, she let herself believe that it was true—that he'd take care of her. Forever.

Eleven

Margaret lay sprawled across William's chest, her body lax and warm in the afterglow of their lovemaking. Will brushed a strand of hair from her face and pressed a kiss to her forehead. He was more grateful to her than she'd probably ever know. Before they'd left his parents' apartment tonight, his dad had taken him aside and told him he was going to start the necessary paperwork to transfer ownership of the farm to Will.

Will had been ecstatic. Finally, he would get his due. And it was all due to the beautiful woman in his arms.

"Thank you," he said softly.

"Mmm? What for, specifically?"

He could feel her smile against his chest and it made him smile even more in return.

"Tonight. For being you."

"Anytime. I enjoyed meeting your family. They're wonderful people."

"They obviously enjoyed meeting you."

She snuggled against him, tracing tiny whorls on his chest. "Being around a family like that again, it reminded me of the good times we used to share with my mom and dad before they died. It reminded me of how much we're missing now that they're gone."

"You were all pretty close, then?"

"Very. Mom and Dad were everything. Our rock, our foundation, our moral compass. They worked really hard so we never went without but they didn't mind teaching us the value of a dollar as well," she said. "Anyway, it was really nice to be a part of a family gathering again, especially one where I wasn't responsible for everything."

Will lay there, at a loss for words. While he loved and appreciated his family, there were times when he begrudged the attention they demanded. Looking at it from Margaret's perspective was a sobering reminder that they wouldn't all be around together forever.

"I like your dad. He seems to be a very upright kind of guy."

"Oh, he is. Upright, opinionated, but always there in our corner when we need someone."

"You're so lucky to still have them in your life, Will. Don't take them for granted."

Will wrapped his arms around Margaret's naked form and gathered her even closer. She sounded so alone and he had no idea how to change that.

"I won't. Not anymore, okay?"

She nodded, her hair tickling his skin as she moved. "At least you've had them supporting you through your formative years. Poor Jason, he only had me and I seem to have made a total mess of him. I wonder how he would have turned out if he'd had a strong male role model in his life. Would he still have gotten into so much trouble?"

"Hey, don't knock it. You did your best." Will tried to comfort her.

"But it wasn't enough, was it? I failed him somewhere."

"Look, the choices he makes as an adult are his own, Margaret. Seriously. You can't be responsible for him and his every move for the rest of his life. At some stage he has to stand up and be a man."

She didn't answer but he could tell she was still thinking about it.

"Margaret, you've done the right thing by him. Don't ever doubt that."

He stroked her silken, soft skin until she fell asleep, her breathing settling into a deep and even pattern. But even as she lay in his arms, he couldn't find the relief of sleep for himself. Her words turned over in his mind. Her fears for her brother—the responsibilities she'd borne for the past ten years. All of it on her own.

Suddenly, he really didn't like what he'd done to her by forcing her to act as his fiancée. He'd taken her weakness, her love for her brother—her sole remaining family—and he'd abused it. He thought about tonight, about how genuinely happy his family had been to see him there with Margaret. To, apparently, be settling in for a long and happy future together.

He'd betrayed them all. From Margaret through to his parents. Even his brothers and their wives, and his unborn nephew. His whole family had embraced Margaret with open arms. Their very generous spirit showing them for the truly loving and supportive family they were. And showing him for the bastard he was to have lied to them the way he had.

Seeing everyone together tonight, knowing the pressure to marry was finally off him, he'd been able to genuinely relax and enjoy the evening. So much so that he could now appreciate what it was that his family strived for him to learn and accept—that all they wanted for him was a share of the love and security that came from relationships such as theirs.

When had he lost sight of what was so important? When had being so darned determined to be the best in the business completely eclipsed the decency with which he was raised?

He looked at himself through new eyes and he didn't like what he saw. Not at all.

As the hours of darkness ticked slowly toward dawn, Will thought long and hard about the type of man he'd become and what he could do to rectify things. It had to start with Margaret. He had to do the gentlemanly thing and let her go—release her from the draconian arrangement he'd browbeaten her into.

Everything inside him told him it was the right thing to do. The only thing to do. And yet, his arms closed even more firmly around the woman in his arms. She made a small sound in her sleep and he eased his hold ever so slightly.

Yes, he'd let her go. But not yet, he decided as he allowed his eyes to slide shut and sleep to overtake his exhausted mind. Not just yet.

When they woke late the next morning, Will wanted to make the most of Margaret's first trip to New York. They didn't have to be at the airport until midafternoon for their flight back to San Diego, so he treated her to a lazy brunch at the Russian Tea Room. As they dined over scrambled eggs and Scottish smoked salmon they talked little, although their casual touches and long gazes said pretty much all they needed to say to one another.

After brunch, they took a short stroll to Central Park where he negotiated an hour-long carriage ride through the park. Having Margaret nestled against him during the ride was a bittersweet joy. They hadn't known each other long, yet he felt so very right with her. When the ride finished and they reluctantly returned to their hotel to collect their luggage and take a car back to the airport, he had the overwhelming sensation that a door was closing on what had possibly been one of the brightest highlights of his life.

Will had a lot of time to think that night, alone in his bed at the Tennis Club. Margaret had insisted on being dropped back home, saying her brother was expecting her. He'd suggested she give Jason a call and let him know she was staying with him, but she'd been adamant.

He thought about Jason Cole. How old was he now? Twenty-four? And still he appeared to be quite dependent upon his sister. Will could understand sibling support, but that went both ways. It seemed that the relationship between Margaret and her brother was very much a one-way affair. Will had no doubt the younger man had been spoiled by his sister, as much as she was able. It wasn't right that Jason should still be molly-coddled at his age. He should be striking out on his own now, at this stage of his life. Being responsible for his own costs and allowing his sister to make her own life, her own way in the world.

Margaret's enjoyment of the trip to New York was the perfect example. She clearly loved to travel and enjoyed seeing new places. Will thought about how he could expand her horizons—show her other, even more exciting places in the world, then reminded himself of his decision to let her go her way.

As he thumped his pillow into shape for the umpteenth time, he reached a decision. It certainly wasn't in his plans to accompany Margaret on the travel he now knew she longed for, but he could swing something to make it easier for her—to free her and allow her to do all those things she'd always wanted to do.

He could indulge in a little man-to-man chat with her

punk brother and give the guy a few pointers in growing up. Satisfied with his plan of action, Will finally drifted off to sleep.

Monday morning he sent a message to Jason Cole, requesting his presence in his office at the end of the workday. Will didn't want to take the risk of brother and sister crossing paths, especially not with what he had to say. Margaret had begged off having dinner with him tonight, saying she had a whole lot of housework to catch up on at home, so he didn't feel guilty when he suggested she leave early for the day. He knew she got a hard time from some of the other staff over early finishes since their engagement had become public knowledge, but he was feeling snarly enough right now that if he overhead anyone say a thing about her, their job would be in jeopardy.

Will was mulling over the report he had to put together about his trip to New Jersey when he heard a knock on his office door.

"Come in," he called, throwing down his pen and closing the file he'd been analyzing.

Jason Cole came through his door and closed it behind him. It was only the second time Will had come face-to-face with Margaret's brother and he was struck by the similarities between them. Although Margaret's features were softer, more rounded, there was no denying the family resemblance between them in coloring and their eyes. Except while Margaret's eyes looked at him softly and with a combination of desire and admiration, Jason Cole's expression left little doubt about his antipathy toward Will.

"Take a seat," Will instructed, getting up from his chair and coming around to the front of his desk. He leaned against the edge of the desk and looked down at Jason who stared straight back at him, not giving so much as an inch. "How's it going, Jason?"

The younger man crossed his arms. "You should know—my supervisor answers to you on a daily basis, doesn't she?"

Will tamped down the anger that instinctively flared at Jason's open disregard for his authority.

"Yes, she does. So far, so good, apparently."

Will's slight hesitation over the last word seemed to act as a catalyst for Jason's anger.

"What the hell do you mean—*apparently?*" he asked belligerently.

"Hey, calm down. Your supervisor has noted your attention to detail and the fact that for the past couple of weeks you've rigidly maintained company operating procedures. I'm pleased to see you've taken this chance to clean up your act."

"I didn't have an act to clean up. I've told you before, and I'll keep saying it until someone believes me. I haven't been defrauding Cameron Enterprises."

Will put up a hand. "Whatever. I'm glad to see that you're shaping up. There's one other area, though, where you're still sadly remiss."

Jason rolled his eyes. "Look, if you're looking for an excuse to fire me—"

"No, this isn't work related."

Ah, he definitely had Jason's attention now.

"What is it, then?"

"It's about Margaret."

"Maggie? What do you mean? I hardly see her anymore, no thanks to you."

"Yet she still feels she needs to be there for you, Jason."

"Of course she does. She's my big sister. Don't you have older siblings who always try to tell you what to do? Do they let you make your own decisions all the time?"

Jason's words fell painfully close to the mark, enough to put Will on the attack again.

"Tell me, exactly when are you going to take responsibility for your own actions? Stand on your own two feet without your sister either bailing you out or protecting you from harm? She's put her entire life on hold for you. Given up opportunities that might never come her way again, for you."

"Do you think I don't know that? Why do you think I'm working so hard here to help her financially?"

"I don't know what to think when it comes to you, Jason. From here you look and act like a spoiled brat. You need to let her go, let her be herself."

"Oh, that's rich, coming from you."

Jason got up from his chair and started to pace the office.

Will's back stiffened. "I beg your pardon," he said, his voice clinically cold.

"What I mean is that at least I'm not actively using her in a lie, like you are. I love my sister. I'd do anything for her, which is a heck of a lot more than you can say. Oh, sure, you have your money and you can give her nice things and take her to exciting places, but at the end of the day, where does she come? Home, that's where. Because despite everything we've been through, she loves me and she knows I love her."

A solid lump choked in Will's throat. There was no way he could refute what Jason had said. In fact, his words spoke volumes as to the relationship brother and sister shared.

"And because I love her," Jason continued, "I would never deliberately do anything to hurt her—like cheat my employer. I think I have evidence as to who actually did cheat Cameron Enterprises, though. *If* you're interested in the truth, that is."

The challenge lay between the two men. A gauntlet hovering on the air.

"What kind of proof?" Will asked.

He didn't believe Jason for a minute, no matter how

impassioned his speech about his love for Margaret. He knew for a fact that when there was smoke, there was generally fire.

Jason reached into the back pocket of his pants and took out a folded sheet of paper.

"It's all there."

He handed the paper to Will and explained his neat notations on the printout. Will's inner sense of order sprang to the fore. Jason's notes did show that he appeared to be onto something. Even so, if he was clever enough to present the information this way, he was probably creative enough to have generated a false trail, as well. Still, it was enough to send up a flag in Will's mind. A flag that sent the analytical side of his brain into overdrive.

"What do you think?" Jason asked.

"I think this is definitely worth investigating further," Will said carefully. "Thank you for bringing it to my attention. Can I ask whether you were actually going to do that any time soon, or did our meeting precipitate it?"

"I wanted to be certain first. When you summoned for me today I thought now was as good a time as any."

"Have you told anyone else about your findings?"

"No, I needed to be sure."

"Good man. Give me your cell number. I might need to call you outside work for more information."

Jason gave Will his number. Will entered it into his phone and then told Jason he could go. He was surprised when the younger man stayed in the same position.

"Problem?" he asked.

"No, not exactly. Just something I need to say."

"Well, then, spit it out."

"Don't hurt my sister."

The words sounded simple enough, but there was sufficient

fire in Jason's eyes for Will to know without a shadow of a doubt that Margaret's brother meant every syllable.

"I won't," he answered.

After Jason left, Will sat for several hours at his desk, his fingers flying over the keys of his laptop or alternately tracing rows of figures. By the time he was finished, he knew the truth. A truth that should have made him rejoice, yet only served to underline what a complete and utter bastard he'd been. He'd seen only what he'd wanted to see. Seen what he could use to his own advantage. But now his blinders had been ripped off. The information he had now gathered was irrefutable.

Jason Cole was innocent.

Twelve

Things had been hectic in the office since their return from New York. Margaret had begun to sense a distance in Will that she couldn't quite put her finger on. In the office he was still the same focused and detail-oriented boss she'd come to expect. Even if they hadn't become lovers she would have enjoyed working with him. He challenged her on many levels, lifting her own abilities so that she could now approach several different tasks with a confidence she'd never known before.

And yet when it came to their personal time together, things were different. They didn't go out as much in the evenings as they had in the beginning. Will seemed content to cook for her in the compact kitchen of his beachfront suite or to order in from one of the Tennis Club's restaurants. In many ways she felt as if he was just marking time, and it bothered her.

She forced the niggling thoughts to the back of her mind and concentrated on the incoming courier package that had arrived from Will's New York office a few minutes ago. As she logged and prioritized each missive, her attention was drawn to a bound report. The date on the cover coincided with the weekend she and Will had spent in New York. Was this related to the hours he'd left her alone at the hotel? Curious, she thumbed through the pages.

Her curiosity didn't last long. Instead, she became filled with a deep sense of dread. The report was a clinical account of a facility in New Jersey, which in itself wasn't so unusual. What was unusual though, was the comparative statement on productivity and costings—comparative with the Vista del Mar branch of Cameron Enterprises. Margaret's eyes scanned the figures, every line making her stomach twist with fear, but the written testimony from Will was what horrified her the most.

For all intents and purposes, the report read like a recommendation to close down the Vista del Mar facility and to relocate the factory work to New Jersey. Margaret closed the report with shaking hands. No wonder Will hadn't wanted her to come along for the trip to New Jersey. He'd had another agenda all along.

Without a second thought, Margaret got up from her chair and took the report into Will's office, entering without even knocking on the door.

"Could you explain this to me?" she asked as she slammed his office door behind her.

The beginnings of a fury like nothing she'd ever known permeated every cell in her body.

"Ah, it's arrived," Will commented.

"Yes, it's arrived. How could you do this?"

"Margaret, it's just a report. Calm down."

"Calm down? No, I won't calm down. Do you have any idea of what this will do to the people here when you recommend to Mr. Cameron that he shut the factory down? This won't just

destroy the lives of everyone who works here, it will destroy
Vista del Mar altogether."

Will got up from his desk and walked over to Margaret,
taking the report from her and throwing it on the desk behind
him before taking her hands in his.

"You're overreacting."

"No, I'm not. I thought you were better than this, Will.
I thought you had begun to really have an interest in
protecting the people who've worked here—some of them
for generations! If you do this you will not only break the
hearts of hundreds of people, you'll destroy any sense of hope
for the young people who live here. Cameron Enterprises is
the major employer for miles around here. If we close down,
communities will be ripped apart when everyone has to leave
the area to find work."

"People move away from home all the time," Will said, his
voice unnaturally calm given her temper.

"Not here. Not in Vista del Mar. We're old-fashioned.
We look after our own. We believe in the core of family
and giving kids grandparents and extended family to grow
up with. Not everyone and everything is about the mighty
dollar."

"Worth Industries has been bleeding money for years. Why
else would Cameron Enterprises have even bought them out—
have you asked yourself that?"

"Then there must be another way. A better way. You're the
brainiac in these matters. Find a solution," she implored.

"This is the simplest solution to offer. The simplest and the
most cost effective. It's there in black and white."

Margaret shook her head. "I know what's in the report,
Will. I've read it and, more importantly, I understand it. But
there has to be another way."

When he didn't respond, she yanked her hands from his.

"I can't believe I misjudged you so badly," she said bitterly.

"You're not the man I thought you were. I thought you prized loyalty."

"I do."

"Then why this?"

"Emotions are not a part of the equation."

"Emotions are everything in the equation. Emotions equate to people. Real people, not numbers. If you go ahead with this recommendation you're nothing better than a cold-blooded, heartless corporate raider like Rafe Cameron. You came here, you saw nothing about the heart of Vista del Mar, and now you'll just head on back to your structured world in New York. Where's your compassion? Did you *ever* have any?"

Margaret stared at the man she loved and realized she didn't know him at all. He stood there in front of her. Every inch of him familiar to her yet she still had no idea who William Tanner, the man, was.

She watched as he pushed a hand through his hair and sighed.

"Look, I know you're upset about this, but you have to understand that I was brought here to do an in-depth analysis of Worth Industries' financial position and make recommendations based on those findings. To do anything less would mean I'm not doing my job to the best of my ability."

"Damn your ability," she said softly, tears now burning in the backs of her eyes.

Will was shocked by how much it hurt to know he'd angered and upset Margaret so profoundly. Even worse was knowing how much he'd dropped in her estimation. He hadn't understood just how much her opinion of him mattered, or how important it was to him deep down.

He knew the results of the report wouldn't be met with any level of joy from the Board of Directors. No one liked the prospect of making so many workers jobless, no matter the economic climate, but the bottom line was as clear as the distress on Margaret's face.

"It's a preliminary report, Margaret. There's no guarantee that Rafe will go ahead with it."

"But it's more than likely, isn't it?"

He nodded. He couldn't lie to her. Not about this. Not when it affected her so completely. She was shaking her head as if she couldn't quite believe it. Will reached out to touch her again but she stepped just out of his reach.

"Don't, please," she said, her voice trembling.

"Don't? I'm simply doing my job."

"I just don't think I can be around you right now."

"Right now, or ever?"

Her eyes flew up to meet his, surprise on her face. "I…I don't know. I need to think about it. I need to go."

He watched in silence as she turned and left his office. For the balance of the day she remained aloof. Answering his questions when he posed them, yet not offering anything but the bare minimum in response.

By the end of their working day he knew what he needed to do. It was something he'd known needed to be done since New York, yet he'd been unable to bring himself to do it—to break that link between them and give her back her life. Now, with Margaret's opinion of him shattered, it would be so much easier to follow through. To do what was best for her. Granted, if the decision to close down the Vista del Mar location became a reality, then she'd be out of a job along with all the rest of them, including her brother. But they were both bright and intelligent individuals. He'd see to it that they were offered work elsewhere through his contacts. It was the least he could do for them both, long-term.

Short-term, however, it was time to release Margaret from

their agreement, but first he needed to make a very important call. To his dad.

Margaret had left the office for the day by the time Will finished his call to his father. He felt completely hollow inside. While his dad had been angry with him for his deliberate deception, he'd appeared to be even more disappointed about the fact that his relationship with Margaret had not been real. Will grabbed an antacid from his top drawer and chewed it down to try and relieve the burning in his gut. He'd damaged and hurt so many people—and for what? A piece of land he personally had no intention of living on or farming? His father was probably already giving the green light to list the property to the realtor he'd kept hanging for the past year. The very idea made him feel as if his heart were being cut out. But he couldn't have continued with the lie.

All those generations of Tanners he'd wanted to revere and remember—the hard-working men and women whose ethics had been as strong as their dream for their land—he'd disrespected them all with his single-minded behavior.

It would be a while before he could mend the fences with his family. Already his cell was buzzing with messages from his brothers, demanding to know if it was true. He'd sunk to his lowest ebb. There was one more thing to do and the sooner he faced it, the better.

The drive to the quaint home where Margaret and Jason lived was short and when he pulled up outside, he waited inside his car for a few minutes. Even though he knew he had to do this, every part of him railed at having to go through with it. He couldn't understand it. They'd had an agreement. Margaret had honored every letter of it. He was the one who had been in the wrong. Letting her go should be easy.

With renewed resolve, Will got out of the car and crossed the pavement to the narrow path leading to her front door. He knocked firmly and waited. Inside, he heard footsteps approaching and his heart rate increased incrementally. Margaret couldn't hide the surprise in her eyes when she opened the door and saw him standing there.

"Will? What are you doing here?"

"There's something I need to tell you."

"Do you want to come inside?"

Even though she'd made the invitation, her voice lacked the warmth he'd come to associate with her.

"No, it's all right. I can say what I have to say here as well as anywhere."

She waited patiently, one hand still holding the door, the other wrapped across her stomach as if bracing for something bad. Will took a deep breath.

"In light of your reaction this afternoon, I'm releasing you from our agreement. You no longer have to pretend to be my fiancée. I don't think it fair or reasonable for you to have to continue with something, or someone, that you obviously find so abhorrent."

She paled, but remained silent. He could see the steady throb of her pulse in the smooth pale column of her throat and had to push down the urge to lean forward and kiss her right there. That was no longer his right. Finally she spoke.

"I see. But what about the farm?"

"I've spoken to my father and told him the truth. He's not happy, but we'll work through it."

"I'm sorry to hear that." Her voice was stilted, unsure. She took a deep breath. "So, us, everything. It was all a complete waste of time. You've just given it all away."

It wasn't like that, he wanted to tell her, but he simply nodded. "For the duration of my work here at Vista del Mar I'd like you to stay on as my assistant, if you're okay with that."

Hell, why had he said that? Back in the office he'd already decided that continuing to work with her, seeing her up close every single day would be torture. He'd already written a letter of recommendation that she take on an EA role elsewhere in the firm. For as long as there remained a firm, that is. But, he faced the daunting truth, he couldn't let her go—not entirely—no matter how good his intentions.

"Of course. Why wouldn't I be?" Margaret responded coolly. "And Jason, is his job still safe, too?"

Of course she'd think of her brother before anything else.

"For now. By the way, I've reopened the investigation into Jason's case at work."

Margaret's lips parted on a gasp and her hand fisted at her chest. "Really?"

"He presented a very convincing argument to me and I've done a little more work on it. It looks as though your brother was telling the truth," Will admitted.

"So he's innocent?"

"It's not proven yet, but it's looking that way."

"That's fantastic. How long have you known?"

"A few days. We'll have the true culprit identified soon, I hope."

"A few days? And neither of you thought to tell me?"

"What difference would it have made?"

Will looked at her, watching the emotions that flew across her beautiful face, clouding her dark brown eyes. Would she have been the one to renege on their agreement first, if she'd known?

"Difference? All the difference in the world. I don't know how you could even ask me that. You have no idea the toll this has taken on me, thinking my brother was a thief."

And the toll sleeping with him had taken on her? What about that? Had every moment been purely for her brother's sake? He'd never know now. Feeling unaccountably empty inside, Will took a step away from the front door. "Well, I'll head off."

"Wait."

Will felt a small kernel of something bloom ever so briefly in his chest until he saw her working the engagement ring he'd given her off her finger.

"Here." She handed it to him. "I won't need this anymore."

He looked at the ring in the palm of his hand and felt a cold lump expand and solidify somewhere in the region of his chest.

"You can keep it if you like."

"No, I don't want it. Really."

Her voice was so detached. Where was the warm and deeply affectionate woman he'd come to know? Had she lost all respect for him over that stupid report?

He shoved the ring into his pocket, not wanting to look at it for another second and certainly not wanting to examine why he felt so suddenly bereft over her returning it. It wasn't as if they had truly been engaged or as if his emotions had been involved.

"I'll see you in the office on Monday, then," he said before turning to walk back to his car.

Behind him the front door slammed closed, the echo of it resounding in his ears—the finality of the sound altogether too real.

The second she shut the door behind him Margaret sank to her knees—her entire body shaking, wretched sobs ripping free from her chest. How she'd held it together while they'd talked she'd never know. It was only once the cold tile floor began to make her knees ache that she struggled upright again.

Thank goodness Jason hadn't been home to witness her breakdown, she thought as she headed to her bathroom to repair the damage to her makeup before he arrived in from the overtime he was so involved with.

She looked at her reflection in the mirror. Outwardly, she looked no different, yet inside she hurt so very much.

Margaret closed her eyes. She'd hoped against hope that Will could have really heard what she'd said to him this afternoon. That he'd have been able to look into his heart and really think about how he presented that report. But it looked as if her heartfelt plea had been in vain. As had been her ridiculous love for him.

Pain rent her anew, and her eyes burned bright with a fresh wash of tears. She had to gather some semblance of control. She'd done it before, in the awful dark days after her parents had died. She could do it again. Bit by bit, piece by piece, put herself back together again and learn to function as if nothing had happened. Grief was something you kept deep inside because if you didn't, it would consume you whole.

She'd known all along that she and Will were not a forever thing. No matter that he'd touched her heart in such a way that she knew she'd never love another the same again. No matter that she'd shared her mind and her body with him in ways she'd always dreamed of. There'd been no foundation to their pretense. They'd been two adults who had come together with no illusions or promises between them.

That she was stupid enough not to be able to keep her mind separate from her heart was her own cross to bear. He, it seemed, had no such difficulty. She doubted she'd even touched his emotions. The way he'd ended their arrangement just now was a perfect example of that. And the way he'd just walked away from the very thing he said he'd wanted most left her head reeling.

The fact that he'd given up his rightful inheritance so easily didn't augur well for the factory. She'd thought he was a better man than that. She'd believed longevity and loyalty had really counted in his world. How wrong she'd been.

She forced her eyes open and looked herself square in the eye. She'd known from the start that it was all make-believe, just as she'd known that when it was over, her heart would be irreparably broken. Now she needed to call on past reserves of strength to find some way to get on with it and to keep working with Will as if breaking off their fake engagement hadn't been the worst thing that had happened to her since her parents died.

In the house she heard the sound of a key turning in the lock at the front door. She rapidly washed her face and threw on a light application of makeup, just enough to create a mask of normality for when she faced her brother. She was the grand master at putting on a brave face. Ten years of hard work at it couldn't have been all for nothing.

She should have known her efforts were in vain.

"What happened?" Jason asked the instant he saw her.

"It's nothing," she said, shaking her head and hoping against hope that he'd leave it at that.

"It doesn't look like nothing. Tell me, Maggie. What is it?"

"Oh, just that I've gone and done the stupidest thing in my entire life," she said, her voice breaking.

Jason looked ill at ease in the face of her raw emotion.

"Don't worry, I'll get over it," she hastened to add. "You know me. Tough as nails."

Jason shook his head. "Get over *him*, you mean."

Margaret swallowed against the lump in her throat. Under Jason's inquiring eyes she could only nod.

"Ah, Maggie. Why did you have to go and fall in love with him?"

Jason held his arms open and Margaret walked into them,

taking comfort in the strength of his hug. It felt strange to have their roles reversed.

"I couldn't help it, Jason. I just did."

They stood there for ages, just holding one another, giving and receiving comfort. Eventually Margaret pulled free from her brother's caring embrace.

"Thank you."

"For what?"

"Not saying, 'I told you so,' about him using me."

Jason just shook his head. "You're a big girl now, Maggie. But it's about time you started to make your own mistakes instead of constantly picking up after mine."

"What do you mean?"

"You need a life of your own. You've been so devoted to me and to making sure that our lives have gone on as close to normal as possible to before that you've completely forgotten to take time out for you. Maggie Cole got lost somewhere along the line."

"I love you, Jason. I couldn't let Mom and Dad down. I had to step up to the plate for you with them gone."

"I know you did, and I appreciate everything you've done for me. Especially for giving up your own college dreams for me to go instead. But…" He grimaced. "I stopped *needing* you a long time ago. I'm twenty-four, Maggie. I have to stand on my own two feet and you have to let me."

Fresh tears sprang to her eyes, but she valiantly blinked them back. He was right. She'd put her life on hold to support him and she hadn't known when to stop. As a result she'd risked suffocating him. It was a miracle she hadn't already.

"Okay, I understand. It might take me a while." She smiled. "But I'll do it. By the way, Will tells me that you might be cleared of wrongdoing in the fraud investigation. Why didn't you tell me?"

Her voice rose a little, showing some of her frustration at

being kept in the dark. After all the subterfuge from Will, was it too much to have expected her brother to have included her in what was happening? After all, it had directly affected her, too.

"He asked me to keep it to myself until we could identify the real culprit."

"I'm so sorry I doubted you. I just—"

"I know," Jason interrupted. "I programmed you to distrust me. But now maybe we can both take a new step forward."

"Definitely," she answered, pasting on a smile for her younger brother's benefit.

Because no matter how many new steps forward she took with her brother, she'd still be without the one person who meant more to her than she'd ever believed possible. Will Tanner.

Thirteen

Telling her their arrangement was over had nothing on the past few days, Will thought to himself as he watched the sway of Margaret's hips as she left his office with the work he'd just given her. He shifted slightly in his seat to ease the discomfort in his groin. The discomfort that despite every command known to man, paid no attention to him and ridiculously leaped to attention every time she was within a few feet of him.

She seemed to suffer under no such difficulty, he noted with a degree of irritation. Each day she serenely sat at her desk, turning out work of an exemplary level without so much as an error or transposition of characters anywhere. It was as if they'd never happened. As if the passion between them had never existed.

He should have been relieved. After all, he'd extricated himself from enough relationships to know that her response to this was indeed a blessing—especially as they continued to work together. But there was a part of him that had begun to sorely regret releasing her from their agreement. He knew it had been the right thing to do, but for the first time in his life the right thing had never felt so utterly wrong.

He missed her. There, he'd admitted it. He missed her in his bed—in his life. Sure, they shared office space, but it was as if she operated inside a protective bubble—immune to all around her. The elements that he'd grown to enjoy most about her—her humor, her wonder in things that were new, her ability to give and give—were now extinguished.

The office had become a somber place to be. The report he'd put in to Rafe and the Board had been met with some serious discussion. The general consensus, though, had been to accept his recommendations, and as if they'd sensed the writing on the wall, there had been a distinct rise in the ill feeling directed toward him by the staff since then. It was a good thing he had broad shoulders, he thought to himself.

It was just before lunchtime that Margaret came marching into his office. Her face more animated than he'd seen it in days—albeit the animation was, once again, anger. Anger directed squarely at him.

She threw a sheaf of papers onto the desk in front of him.

"What kind of game are you playing?" she demanded.

Will put down his pen and leaned back in his chair. "Care to explain your question?"

"This." She gestured to the scattered papers. "You're recommending the complete opposite of the last report. Are you trying to commit career suicide? Don't you know that you probably risk totally alienating your boss with this? From what I understand, Rafe Cameron is determined to dismantle what's left of Worth Industries no matter what—even if a more profitable solution for us can be found. He certainly seemed keen enough to adopt your last report. Why are you even bothering with this one?"

He shrugged. "The report is what it is. I've compiled my most recent findings and presented them here." He tapped the papers. "Are you telling me you disagree with my recommendation again?"

"Of course I'm not, but why didn't you say this the first time around?"

Will leaned back in his chair and tucked his hands behind his head. "I didn't have all the information at my disposal. Now I do. The other report was a preliminary finding. Obviously, since then, I've gleaned further information. I'm meeting with Rafe tonight to discuss it. I really think the factory is viable if, and that's a big if, they make product changes and convert the factory for a more specialized high-tech use.

"Sure, it's going to cost Cameron Enterprises a few cool million in updating the factory and continuing education for the staff, but long-term the gains will be huge. I'm hoping that'll be the carrot that secures Rafe's interest, besides the fact that doing this will ensure the community remains economically healthy with, hopefully, an even higher level of employment than Vista del Mar currently enjoys."

Margaret just stood there looking at him as if he'd grown two heads. Eventually, she spoke.

"So you're seriously going to pursue this avenue? It'll mean everything to the staff here if it can go ahead. Lately everyone's just been walking around as if they're waiting for a guillotine to fall. Morale has been terrible," Margaret commented. "Do you really think he'll go for it?"

"No, probably not. But I couldn't let this pass without bringing it to his attention." He leaned forward and gathered up the papers. "Much as I appreciate the speed with which you've transcribed this, I don't think I can give it to Rafe looking like this. I don't want him to have any excuse to trash it before he's even read the contents."

She reached forward and snatched them from him. "Don't worry," she said. "They will be perfectly bound and back on your desk in ten minutes."

Margaret went home later that day completely unsure of how she should be feeling. She was afraid to hope that Rafe Cameron would accept Will's current proposal. Sure, on paper it all made sense and the forward projections were almost embarrassingly promising. But would Cameron go for it? It was pretty clear now that he'd had some agenda against Worth Industries long before he'd come back. Gillian's acerbic editorials in the *Gazette* had probed his every decision for all to see. You couldn't even go to the grocery store without overhearing people questioning his motives. No matter how much effort he was seen putting into Hannah's Hope, everyone still suspected it was a smoke screen for whatever it was that he really planned to accomplish. And right now that seemed to be the total decimation of the only business that had kept the town alive. She doubted he'd even give Will's new proposal the time of day, no matter how prudent the recommendations.

The thing that struck her most about today was Will's total apparent commitment to this new course of action for the company. He was prepared to go head-to-head with Rafe Cameron over the whole thing, even knowing that his proposal was unlikely to be adopted. Maybe she'd made a terrible mistake in judgment about him after all. She'd been so quick to accuse him of being a corporate raider just like his boss. Wondering whether she'd gotten the completely wrong idea about him didn't sit well with her. Nor did the awareness that he'd let her go on thinking that way.

Would she have listened to him? Let him persuade her

thinking back his way? Or had he just been looking for a reason to end their arrangement—perhaps had wearied of her? She still didn't understand his about-face on the farmland he'd talked about with such enthusiasm. It had meant so much to him on so many levels, and yet he'd let it go, just like that. It just didn't make any sense.

Margaret went through the motions of preparing dinner for herself and Jason even though she'd had no appetite for anything lately. She was just about to remove the chicken cacciatore from the oven when she heard the roar of Jason's motorbike coming up the driveway. She straightened as she heard the front door bang open on its hinges and the sound of Jason's feet swiftly moving through the house.

"What's wrong?" she asked as he came into the kitchen.

In response, he wrapped his arms around her and swung her in a circle until she was dizzy.

"Nothing's wrong," he shouted happily. "Everything couldn't be more right!"

Margaret laughed as Jason set her back on her feet and she put a hand out on a nearby chair back to steady herself.

"Wow, what brought that on?"

She looked at her brother's face. He hadn't been this animated since he'd graduated college. For a second her heart squeezed. Right now he looked so much like their father with his big happy smile and dancing eyes.

"Good news. No, *great* news."

"So tell me already," she coaxed, still laughing.

"I've been cleared. Exonerated. Acquitted and, most important, vindicated, from all wrongdoing."

"Jason, that's wonderful news! I'm so happy for you. I should never, ever have doubted you."

Unexpected tears filled her eyes and started to spill down her cheeks.

"Ah, Maggie," he said gruffly, pulling her into his arms

for a massive bear hug. "It's okay. I know I wasn't always an angel, but I meant it outside the courthouse the last time, when I said I would never let you down like that again. I guess from now on you'll believe me, huh?"

She nodded and sniffed, pulling from his arms and searching out a paper towel to wipe her face dry.

"I didn't mean to get all blubbery on you. I'm sorry. This is great news, so that makes these happy tears, okay?"

"Sure, whatever you say." Jason grinned back.

"So tell me what happened," Margaret said, reaching for her oven mitts. She took the chicken dish from the oven and ladled it onto plates.

"It was awesome," Jason enthused. "She didn't know it, but we had her neck in a noose."

"She? Your supervisor?"

"Yep. She's being grilled by Tanner now. From what we can tell, there's a whole lot more that she's been dipping her fingers into than what she tried to pin on me."

"That's terrible. And to think she was ready to let you take the blame for all that."

Margaret added steamed green beans to their plates and took them to the table. Jason readily sat down and picked up his fork.

"And that's not all," he said, gesticulating with his fork. "Tanner commended me for my forensic accounting skills in uncovering the clues that led to the real culprit. You know, he might come across tough as nails, but deep down he does seem to care about people, doesn't he? I mean, he was all staunch and tough on me when he thought I was in the wrong, but he was still man enough to shake my hand and apologize when he knew I wasn't."

The bite of chicken she'd just swallowed stuck in her throat and Margaret reached for her water glass to help swallow it. Now Jason was in the Will Tanner fan club? The irony would have been funny if it wasn't so unbearably painful. The way Jason had described Will was spot-on.

When she didn't speak, Jason continued, "You know, I was wrong about Tanner's motives. He really does have our best interests at heart. I'm sorry I was so down on the two of you and you helping him out the way you did."

"Don't worry about it," Margaret managed to say. "That's all over now, anyway, except for the EA role."

Jason shot her a sharp glance, but she was relieved when he didn't press for more.

"He's gone the full distance for me in this, Maggie. He's recommended to the head of my division that I be offered a company scholarship to go back to school and specialize in forensic accounting, since I seem to have a knack for it. Natural aptitude is what he said. Reckons I'll be an asset to the company in the long term."

Margaret could barely believe her ears. Somehow she must have said the right words and Jason, thank goodness, carried most of the rest of the conversation in his excitement at the new opportunities opening up for him. But had she heard him right? Was this the same William Tanner who'd manipulated the situation with Jason to coerce her into his arms and into his bed?

She had to admit that sleeping with Will was a choice she'd made on her own, but she was completely overwhelmed by what the day had brought. First the new proposal, and now this? It was almost too much to take in. As much as she was thrilled for Jason and his future prospects, what would happen to them if the factory was forced to close their doors and cease operations?

Either way, William Tanner would eventually head back to New York or whatever role Rafe Cameron had lined up for him next. And no matter how much she wished otherwise, he'd be taking her fractured heart with him.

When Jason offered to clean up after their meal she didn't argue, which earned her a concerned look from her brother. And when she said she was heading off to bed for an early night he looked even more worried. But she couldn't find the energy to tell him she was okay. Not when she faced another night lying in her bed, alone, staring at the ceiling and wondering how on earth she was going to get through the next day.

Will stepped out onto his terrace facing the ocean and sank into one of the chairs, nursing a shot of whiskey in a tumbler between his hands. He stared out over the darkened ocean as exhaustion dragged at his body. What a day.

Normally a day like today would have seen him pumped to the max, exhilaration oozing from every pore, and yet he felt flat. The meeting with Rafe had been short and sweet and to the point but Rafe had kept his cards close to his chest, refusing to make a decision at this stage of the game. And in many ways it was a game to him. The guy literally was a rags-to-riches story of success. Which made his fixation on Worth Industries all the more intriguing.

Not for the first time, Will wondered what drove a man like Rafe. The guy had lost his mom at a fairly young age and his dad had later remarried. For a couple of minutes Will tried to dwell on what it would have been like to lose either of his parents while he was still a kid. There was no doubting it would have a monumental effect on anyone.

Rafe was currently living in a spectacular property overlooking the beach. The condo had cost a pretty penny and Rafe had commented on it being a far cry from what he'd grown up in. And yet, he was probably on his own at this very moment. Alone like Will was himself.

In fact, he'd never felt more alone.

Deep inside there was a hollow emptiness that he couldn't

ignore. Outwardly, he had everything he'd ever wanted. He had his apartment in Manhattan, a job he loved. Challenges every day that tested his mental acuity and ability to its fullest extent.

He should be on top of his game right now. He'd done a bloody good job on the Worth Industries takeover and proposals and, with Jason Cole's assistance, uncovered who had been acting outside of company procedure for pecuniary gain. So why then did he lack the sense of satisfaction that usually accompanied a job well done? The "rightness" about his work. Something was very definitely missing.

Will took a sip of the whiskey and swallowed it slowly, feeling the burn all the way down to his stomach. Who was he kidding? Of course he was missing something. Margaret. Just thinking her name was enough to sharpen the ache he felt deep inside. Not having her with him, not seeing her smile or hearing the sound of her voice, not feeling the softness of her welcoming body beneath him.

Will put his drink down on the table in front of him and stared at the glass. He'd never felt this way about a woman before. Somehow, Margaret had become as integral to his every day as breathing. She was his first thought on waking, his last on going to sleep and she infiltrated his dreams with recurring frequency. He'd royally screwed up.

They'd shared a powerful attraction back in February and he'd acted on it as he acted on everything—with determination to achieve his ultimate goal. So what was his ultimate goal now? He'd told himself he needed to use Margaret to get his dad to sign over the family farm, but even he hadn't been able to stand himself any longer when he'd analyzed how horribly he'd used her and deceived his family. The end had never justified the means.

He was left with less than nothing. His brothers had left curt messages on his cell phone and his mother hadn't even been in contact with him since Will's discussion with his father. He'd hurt them all so badly, but, he suspected, none as badly as he'd hurt Margaret. He'd lowered her importance in his world to nothing less than a pawn in an intricate game of chess. A vital piece on the playing board, yet sacrificial at the same time.

He'd been a prize fool. He'd sabotaged what had the potential to be the best thing he'd ever had, and he'd done it all himself. Finally he could begin to understand where his family was coming from. What they wanted for him. He'd been on the verge of having that with Margaret, and he'd ruined everything.

Now he could understand why he'd been so reluctant to end their affair. She'd begun to mean more to him than anyone or anything he'd ever loved before.

Will sat up straight in his chair.

Loved? He loved Margaret Cole. The words turned around in his mind, over and over, as if he couldn't quite believe them. He said it out loud.

"I love Margaret Cole."

The hollowness in his chest began to ease, so he said it again, even louder, and then again, in a shout that attracted the attention of a couple strolling on the darkened shoreline in front of the hotel.

He loved Margaret Cole with the kind of love that came from deep inside him. So deep even he had not wanted to reach that far to examine how she made him feel. How much he wanted, no, *needed* her at his side, in his life, forever. In his pigheadedness he'd done a huge amount of damage but he hadn't gotten where he was today by giving up at the first, or even the highest, hurdle.

Forgetting all about the almost untouched whiskey he'd left on the patio table, he went back into his suite, grabbed a jacket and his car keys from his bedroom and went out through the door at a run. He couldn't waste another moment. He had to try to mend things between them now.

As he drove to Margaret's home, he thought about the things his family had wanted for him and yet he'd been too stubborn and too darn focused on work to ever believe that kind of love could have a place in his life. Now he knew his life was all the more empty, that he was only half a man, without it.

He turned onto her street and felt the first seeds of doubt. The sensation was foreign to him. Usually he could bank on the outcome of any situation he instigated but this wasn't something he could define with numbers. It wasn't assets or liabilities, or profit or loss. It was a fearful thing he couldn't quantify in any shape or form.

Will pulled up at the curbside and turned off his engine, staying seated in the darkened interior of his car. This was crazy. He'd come without warning, without even knowing if she reciprocated his feelings. Logically, sure, he knew she had to have some feelings for him. A woman like Margaret wasn't the type who'd embark on a sexual affair at the drop of a hat with a man she barely knew. He replayed some of their time together through his mind—the moments where she'd seemed at her happiest. The moment, in particular, when he'd given her the ruby and diamond ring. Happy, and yet pensive at the same time. She'd had so many moments like that, and if he thought about it properly, there'd been a yearning in her eyes. Maybe he was only grasping at straws but the idea gave him a glimpse of hope. Hope he probably wasn't entitled to feel given his behavior in forcing her to be with him. Could he honestly expect Margaret to believe him when he told her he loved her? Could he even dream to hear the same in return?

There was only one way to find out. Will got out of the car and strode to the front door of the modest home. There was no porch light on and he hesitated before knocking. It was late, maybe she was asleep already. Well, she'd have to wake up. This was far too important to wait until tomorrow.

He knocked sharply on the door and waited. Footsteps on the other side signaled that someone at least was home and awake. The door opened, revealing Jason on the other side.

"Mr. Tanner. What—?" he started.

"Is Margaret home?"

"Yes, she is. She went to bed early, though."

"Jason? Who is it?" Margaret's voice echoed down the hallway.

Will stiffened at the sound of her voice and looked at Jason, who was studying him with a strange expression on his face.

"Maybe I should head out for a bit," Jason said.

"Good idea," Will said, tossing Jason the keys to his car and pushing the key card to his suite into Jason's hand. "Feel free to stay out all night."

He closed the door behind the now smiling younger man at the same moment Margaret came out from a side room—her bedroom, he surmised. The instant she saw him she wrapped her robe tightly around her body, revealing far more of her than she probably hoped to conceal.

Will started to walk toward her.

"We need to talk," he said in a tone that brooked no argument.

Margaret couldn't believe her eyes. Will Tanner, here in her house at this time of night? Even if she'd dreamed it she wouldn't have believed it.

She led him through to the kitchen where she gestured for him to sit down.

"Coffee?" she asked, realizing it was the first thing she'd said to him since his shocking arrival.

"Leave that," he answered as he reached for her hand and tugged her down into the seat next to his.

For a man who'd seemed so intent on a discussion he was being surprisingly quiet. Margaret clutched at straws for something to talk about.

"How did the meeting with Mr. Cameron go?"

Will shrugged. "He said he'll take the recommendations on board but he didn't make any promises."

Margaret sighed, but started as he spoke again.

"I'm not here to talk about work."

"So why, then? That's all we have in common, right?"

"No. That's not all we have in common." He huffed a sigh of frustration. "At least, I hope that's not all we have in common."

She waited patiently, silently, hardly daring to move a muscle as he appeared to pull his thoughts together, his eyes cast down as if he was examining the very grain of the wooden tabletop.

"I'm here because I don't want to be away from you tonight. In fact, I don't want to spend another night without you in my arms—ever."

He looked at her then and she could see it in his eyes. He meant every single word of it. But she wanted more than that. It wasn't enough that he wanted her body. He had to want *her*—mind, body and soul.

"What exactly do you mean by that, Will? Are you asking me to resume the arrangement we had?" she asked cautiously, not even daring to hope for her heart's desire.

"I'm not talking about some half-assed arrangement. I was a complete idiot to even dream that up. I never gave us a chance to be a proper couple. To court you. To show you how much I've grown to love you and to hope that one day you'll also love me in return. I want that opportunity now. I love you, Margaret. I want us to start again."

Margaret's breath caught sharply in her throat. He loved her? Was she dreaming? No, he was definitely here in her kitchen, looking as gorgeous as ever, the scent of his cologne subtly teasing her senses. She looked at him, unsure of what to do or say.

"Margaret, please give me another chance. I don't expect you to return my love straight away. I know I've gone about this all the wrong way but I'm hoping you'll find it in your heart to forgive me for that start and grant me a new one."

"Shh." Margaret laid a finger on Will's lips. "You don't need to say any more. Will, I've loved you pretty much from the moment I first saw you at the ball. I know it sounds stupid and horribly romantic, but I'd never felt such a connection with another person before. When you kissed me, it was as if I was being transported into another world. A world I'd craved ever since I was a little girl. I was afraid to admit that I could feel so much so soon, but when we started our fake engagement I knew I was fighting against the tide. I could never have been with you in San Diego, the way I was, if I didn't love you. I can't believe you love me in return."

"Believe it," Will said gruffly.

He stood and pulled her to her feet, gathering her gently into his arms and tilting her chin up so she looked straight into his face.

"I love you, Margaret Cole. More than I ever thought possible."

When he kissed her, Margaret was instantly assailed with the familiar surge of desire that always accompanied his touch, yet at the same time it was permeated with a sense of rightness, a belonging that had been missing from their liaison before. And when she took his hands and led him down the hall toward her bedroom, she knew she'd be able to finally show him, with all the love within her, exactly how she felt about him—using both words and her touch.

In the darkness of her childhood bedroom, their lips met and melded together again. Margaret's hands deftly slid Will's jacket from his shoulders, before flying to the buttons of his shirt and sliding each one free. As soon as his chest was bare she smoothed her hands over his skin, her hands tingling at the touch, her entire body warming in response. Beneath her palms she felt his nipples grow taut and she relinquished his lips only long enough to press a kiss to each one, swirling the tip of her tongue around each hard male disk, loving the way his body shuddered in response.

He wasted no time disrobing her, her robe soon a jumbled mass of cotton on her bedroom floor. The satin three-quarter pants she wore soon followed, as did the short-sleeved satin shirt. Once she was naked, he pushed her gently onto the bed before shucking his shoes and socks and finally, his jeans and briefs, which he slid off in one smooth rush.

She sighed in contentment as he covered her body with his own, relishing the heat of his skin, the deftness of his touch. And when he brought her to orgasm with his skillful fingers before donning a condom and sliding his length inside her, Margaret felt tears of joy spring to her eyes. Nothing before had ever been like this. Not with him, not with anybody.

They belonged together. In love as in all things.

As Will started to move within her, she met and welcomed each thrust—sensation spiraling tighter and tighter until she let go on a burst of joy so complete she thought she'd lose consciousness. His own climax came simultaneously and as she held him in her arms, feeling his body shake with the strength of his pleasure, she'd never felt so right with her world in all her life.

They lay together, joined, she supporting the weight of his body with her own, for some minutes. Their breaths mingling, the rhythm of their lungs in perfect synchronization. Their heartbeats slowing to a more natural tempo as their skin cooled.

Will shifted, withdrawing from her, and supporting his weight on his elbows. In the shadowed light of her room, Margaret looked up into eyes that gleamed with intent.

"I want you to wear my ring again," he said, his voice a little unsteady but growing stronger with each carefully chosen word. "And one day, when you're ready, I want you to be my wife. Except this time, we'll do everything the right way. In our own time. So, how about it? Will you marry me?"

Marry him? Margaret searched his face, almost too afraid to believe what she was hearing. But it was clear in his eyes, in the expression on his handsome features. He meant every word. She felt the final remnants of the sorrow around her heart begin to melt.

"Yes," she whispered against his lips. "Yes, I will marry you."

As their lips met and as they began to make love again, she knew she'd done the right thing. For today and for all her tomorrows.

The sun caught the gleam of brilliance residing on Margaret's ring finger as they exited Paige Adams's office the next morning. Although she was snowed under with work for the upcoming gala for Hannah's Hope, she'd gleefully agreed to arrange their wedding for the same weekend so all their friends, and Will's family, who'd be in town for the gala, could attend.

Will had scarcely been able to believe that Paige could organize a wedding at such short notice, yet he had to admit, as he looked at the woman on his arm, she'd already proven she had the touch of a fairy godmother about her.

Margaret's fingers squeezed his forearm and he watched as a supremely happy smile spread across her face.

"Happy?" he asked, knowing he already knew her answer.

"I couldn't be happier," she said. "Everything is right with my world. Jason is well and truly on the straight and narrow and I have the one thing I've always wanted my whole life."

"And that is?"

"The love of a very good man. You."

* * * * *

*Travel back to a more innocent time,
when a young Rafe Cameron took his
sweetheart to the prom, long before he became
a ruthless corporate raider.
Turn the page for an exclusive short story by
USA TODAY bestselling author Catherine Mann.
And look for the next installment in
THE TAKEOVER miniseries,
EXPOSED: HER UNDERCOVER MILLIONAIRE
by Michelle Celmer,
wherever Harlequin books are sold.*

Rafe & Sarah—Part Four

CATHERINE MANN

Vista del Mar, California
14 years ago

Sarah Richards saw stars in more ways than one.

Dots sparked in front of her eyes from the camera flash, then began to fade. As she stood with Rafe against the photographer's backdrop, the celestial-themed prom came into focus again. Since she was part of the decorations committee, Sarah had spent most of the school day hanging glow-in-the-dark stars from the ceiling along with luminescent planets and a crescent moon. The whole gymnasium glowed like a sixth-grade science project on steroids.

Hokey? Sure. Even the DJ was over the top in a spaceman suit, with his helmet resting on top of a speaker. But how could the evening be anything other than perfect since she spent it with Rafe?

The photographer snapped his fingers for their attention. "One more shot, just to be sure. Now look here and smile big for the camera."

Rafe's arms tightened around her waist, her hands folded

on top of his, perfectly placed so her wrist corsage showed. She had no idea how Rafe afforded to shower her with so many flowers. When she asked, he always said not to worry. Just enjoy.

And speaking of enjoying. She leaned back against his broad chest, wishing the whole night could last about ten hours longer.

His ribs expanded and she knew he was inhaling the scent of her hair. She'd been sure to put perfume on it since they would be slow dancing. She'd even gotten a new haircut, like Jennifer Aniston, if Jennifer Aniston had red hair. The look was all layered and fell around her shoulders, sort of messed up as if she was always breathless from making out with a guy. Which she was. Her grandmother had pulled two strands back with little fake diamond pins.

The camera flash popped again and the photographer shouted, "Next."

Rafe's arms fell away, his palm landing possessively on the small of her back. Yum! A Spice Girls tune pumped through the speakers as she walked past stacked-up gym mats draped with a solar-system-patterned bed sheet.

As they stepped aside for another couple waiting to have their picture taken, Rafe whispered against her ear. "You're the prettiest girl here."

His compliment stirred a meteor shower in her stomach that beat anything hanging from the rafters. "And you're too hunky in that tux, you know."

He filled out the tuxedo so much better than any other guy in the room. He wore a regular black one, no funky-colored tie to match her seafoam green dress. He looked like some prince or secret agent in his sleek simplicity up next to guys who'd chosen everything from an ice blue jacket to a fuchsia cummerbund.

Glancing at him again, she swallowed hard, her mouth

drying right up. "I'm going for a refill on the punch before we dance again."

"I can get that for you." He slid his arm from her waist.

"I'm a big girl. I can take care of myself, you know."

"Of course you can." He tucked a strand of her loose hair over her shoulder, his knuckles along her collarbone exposed by the spaghetti straps on her dress. "But I'm trying to be a good date here. Don't wreck it for me."

"Only you could figure out a way to make it sound like I'm doing you a favor by letting you do something for me." She tugged his tie straight, keeping an eagle eye out to make sure the PDA police weren't watching. Luckily, the chaperones all seemed plenty busy booting party-crashing college students.

He closed his hand around her wrist, his blue eyes flaming with awareness at her touch. "Do you want the punch or not?"

"Thank you, if you're sure. I wanted to make a request from the DJ, anyway." Something slow so she could stay in Rafe's arms without worrying that the chaperones would have a hissy fit.

She backed toward the DJ table, keeping her eyes on Rafe for as long as she could. He vowed he'd never worn a tux before, but he seemed as at ease in the formal gear as he did in his work clothes. She felt guilty that he'd spent so much money on the evening, but the second she'd hinted that they should skip the whole thing, he'd cut her short. There was no missing how she'd stung his pride by even suggesting it.

She watched as Rafe stopped in front of the refreshments table covered in a midnight blue tablecloth. He reached for one of the plastic cups, holding it up to be filled. Fellow student Margaret Cole stood behind the big clear punch bowl. Margaret was years younger, but teachers were giving out extra credit to anyone willing to help with the prom.

Margaret's little brother, Jason, sat on the floor behind her, leaning against the wall. Ten years old, he played a handheld video game, his backpack beside him. He was young to be out this late, but Margaret rarely went anywhere without her brother in tow. Her parents worked nights, too, sometimes. Where Margaret always did the right thing, her brother Jason was always in trouble. Her parents didn't dare leave the kid alone. Of course, living in a small town where everyone knew everybody helped keep extra eyes on the kid.

Rafe smiled at Margaret, stopping Sarah's thoughts short. She hated the stab of jealousy. She knew deep in her gut that he wasn't interested in the other girl. Still, possessiveness gripped Sarah tighter than the sweaty junior to her left squeezed his giggling girlfriend while they shuffled around the dance floor. She wanted to yank the microphone away from the DJ and shout to the whole gym, "Hey, ladies? Rafe Cameron is all mine. So keep your mitts off him, please."

Of course, doing something like that would be totally juvenile. Not that Margaret would chase Rafe anyhow. The girl was totally into her studies and completely unaware of how pretty she really was behind those glasses and scraggly ponytail.

Rafe turned away from the refreshments. Sarah grabbed a pencil from the DJ table and quickly scrawled her request. She spun back just in time to face her date.

He passed her the cup. "Here you go."

Sipping, she tasted…blue raspberry punch. Yum. "Aren't you going to have any?"

"Water's fine for me." Prisms from the spinning disco ball cast tiny spots of light across his face.

"You don't know what you're missing." She drank again. "Thank you. I feel bad for Margaret, doing so much work and not getting to have any fun."

Rafe glanced back over his shoulder. "She'll make a sharp businesswoman some day."

The admiration in his voice made her eye the refreshment table again. Maybe Margaret needed a guy of her own to help her have fun. Somebody like Quentin Dobbs. It would be nice to make that happen once Margaret was older. Then Sarah would get to see them together over time when she came back to town for visits.

The fact that she and Rafe would actually be leaving in another month still blew her mind—and scared her to her toes. But since she'd started dating him in January, she'd realized the only way to keep him would be to leave town with him.

She drained her drink, set aside the glass and took his strong, calloused hand. "Let's dance. I requested a song for us."

"And that would be?"

"Something slow." The DJ talked through the fade over to the next song…Garth Brooks. She stepped into Rafe's arms, loving the way his hands felt against the small of her back. Heat flooded her and she went lightheaded thinking about later. With Rafe.

He pulled her more firmly against his chest, his cheek against her forehead, his breath warm and sexy in her hair. "I like the way you think."

As much as she wanted this night to last forever, later couldn't come soon enough.

Rafe shifted the car into park on top of Busted Bluff, the highest point that overlooked the town and the Pacific. Finding a halfway secluded spot up here had been tougher than usual since it was prom night, but at least his dad's car had tinted windows. His father's beat up old Chevy Blazer was only marginally better than his own El Camino, but he was all about doing anything he could to make this night as special as possible for Sarah.

He'd wanted to take her to that fancy new restaurant,

Jacques', since their Valentine's plans had been canceled. However, the place was catching on so fast, reservations had to be made far in advance now. Well, unless you were some rich dude like Ronald Worth and could buy yourself a last minute table anywhere. Might as well rename this town Vista del Worth.

So Rafe had moved on to plan B—the steak house. Sarah had ended up eating a salad because she was all freaked out over that Mad Cow Disease scare. As if Vista del Mar could get any nuttier.

He eyed the night sky, already counting down the days until he was out of this Nowhereville, California, town.

Sarah toed off her high heels, kicked them under the seat. "This whole evening has been absolutely perfect."

Her dress rode up to show off slender calves and glittery toenail polish.

He ached to kiss every inch of her. "I'm glad you had fun."

He'd willingly endured the expense and overabundance of crepe paper for her, but if the DJ had played one more Spice Girls song, his head would have exploded. Of course, his cranky mood could have more to do with abstinence than music choices. Taking care of himself in the shower wasn't cutting it anymore, but he wasn't the kind of guy to push a girl if she wasn't ready.

"More than fun. Perfection." Sarah sank deeper into the seat with a sigh that pushed her breasts against the fitted top of her greenish blue dress.

He eyed the spaghetti straps, his fingers aching to nudge them away. Tearing his attention from her, he turned on the radio and searched for an easy-listening station. At least his dad's sound system worked.

Even though it pained him to offer, he said, "We can still go to the after-prom party if you want."

"No, thanks," she answered without hesitation. "I would rather be alone with you."

Thank God. With any luck, she was getting closer to "ready."

"Then we're in agreement." He angled his mouth over hers. Finally, he had her all to himself. She melted against him, her arms looping around his neck as she wriggled to get closer. She tasted like blue raspberry punch and something he couldn't quite pinpoint, but then she usually scrambled his brain.

And the scent of her?

She drove him crazy. He thrust his hands into her hair, the two pins tink-tinking onto the floor. The natural waves curved around his fingers as if binding him closer to her. She tugged at his tie, shoving aside his jacket, her touch more frenetic than usual. He understood one hundred percent. Making out, touching her, was mind-blowing, but also frustrating as hell when he knew it wouldn't play out.

But there was a new edge in her tonight, too, a peeling away of nerves and inhibition that made him wonder if finally, *finally* they could go all the way.

Sarah nipped his bottom lip. "I think the punch was spiked."

Her words all but splashed ice water in his lap.

Pulling back, he looked into her dilated green eyes. "Why do you say that?"

"I'm still seeing stars behind my eyes and we're not at the gym anymore." She crinkled her freckled nose. "And the sky's spinning. God didn't make the moon into a disco ball, did he?"

Ah, hell. He sagged back. "No, Kitten, he didn't."

"Too bad. 'Cause it's really pretty," she said, her voice a little slurred now that he listened more closely rather than staring at her breasts. "And you're really hot in that tux. I dream about you, you know."

He could *not* listen to another word, especially if her dreams were even half as steamy as his own.

"I should take you home." He reached for the ignition.

She gripped his hand. "If you take me home drunk my grandma will kick your ass."

Quite possible, but he was more concerned about Sarah. He pulled her hand gently, but firmly, off his. "You've got quite a mouth when you've been drinking."

"Just because I don't say the words doesn't mean I don't know them." Exhaling in frustration, she picked up her pins one at a time off the floor. "Hell is a useful word. As in, this night sure as hell isn't turning out like I planned right now. But my all-time favorite curse word is sh—"

"That's okay." He stifled a grin. "I've heard it before and I'm betting you'll be embarrassed tomorrow by what's coming out of your mouth tonight."

Her hands slid up his neck. "Then shut me up."

She pressed her lips to his, her tongue thrusting with more enthusiasm than art. His grin faded and his heart rate ramped all over again. Sarah on a regular day tested his self-control. A tipsy Sarah with dwindling inhibitions had his hands shaking.

Without once pulling her mouth from his, she swung her leg over his until she straddled his lap. She wriggled enticingly, her hair falling forward all around him. He wanted her, and he knew she wanted him every bit as much, even when sober. Except she'd been clear she didn't think she was ready to take things to the next level. He was pretty sure she wanted a ring first.

She cupped his crotch.

Her favorite curse word blasted through his brain. He

thought he would explode right then and there, he ached to have her so damn bad.

Not. Cool.

He clamped her wrist. "Sarah, that's enough." As much as it pained him to say it, he had to tell her, "We need to stop."

"I thought you wanted me to touch you." Her hand moved up then down against the fly of his tuxedo pants, cupping and caressing. "Am I doing it right?"

"Uh-huh." His eyes closed and fire-hot want pumped through him, pushing reason to the far corners of his brain. He damn near cracked a crown clenching his jaw.

"I want us to go all the way right here." She whispered exactly what he'd been hoping to hear for so long. "This is the perfect night."

And she was drunk, which made it not perfect. As much as he wanted this, wanted her, he knew it couldn't happen now.

But if he took her home this way, her grandmother would have an absolute fit. Kathleen Richards ruled that family, and oversaw almost every aspect of Sarah's social life since her parents worked the night shift. He would never get to see her again. And even the thought of that made his gut knot.

He scrambled for something, any kind of solution that could salvage this date. He settled on a solution that would take care of her, help him stay in control and keep her family from hitting the roof.

"Come on, babe. We need to get some coffee into you before I take you home."

"I don't want coffee." She tugged down the straps on her dress until the frothy fabric inched dangerously low. "I want more punch and more of you."

The gown fell away from her breasts. His mouth went dry and not a chance in hell could he look away. He'd touched her, stroked her, felt every inch, but *seeing* her? Wow. He didn't have words.

Blood surged south so hard and fast he was quickly losing the ability to think. He needed to put a stop to this ASAP.

Rafe scraped her dress back in place and hauled her off his lap. "Well, Kitten, we don't always get what we want. Come on. We're going to see my dad and Penny."

In Rafe's kitchen, Sarah cradled the mug of coffee, her third, and sipped the kick-butt strong brew. She didn't feel a hundred percent steady yet, but at least the refrigerator had stopped wobbling from side to side. She hadn't wanted him to bring her to his father and his dad's fiancée, Penny, but Rafe had insisted it was here, or go home to face Grandma Kat.

So here she sat in her prom dress, with her corsage wilting as fast as her buzz. "I am *so* embarrassed."

Penny nudged aside the stack of Rafe's textbooks on the table and patted her hand. "It's not your fault someone spiked the punch."

Bob's fiancée was a nice lady, kinda quirky, but Sarah actually liked that about her. And Penny was clearly devoted to Bob. The woman rarely took her eyes off her Harrison Ford look-a-like fiancé.

Bob Cameron turned on the water for a second pot of coffee, then shoved it under the yellowed-with-age maker. "Who would have spiked the punch?"

"My guess?" Rafe leaned against the orange countertop, his tuxedo tie undone and loose. "Jason Cole probably snatched a bottle out of his dad's liquor cabinet. The kid's only ten but I wouldn't put it past him. He's done worse."

Bob shook his head, settling back against the countertop beside his son—who'd grown two inches taller than him. "Sounds a little farfetched, but trouble does follow that kid for sure."

Did the adults believe she hadn't known the punch was spiked? She cringed that they might think she was lying. Their approval was really important to her. These two people would be her family forever once she and Rafe got married.

Would Bob and Penny stay in Vista del Mar? She knew that Bob had been looking for a better job since he got his GED. Her hands trembled around the mug as she thought of everything changing so fast. Would there be anything familiar to return to here?

The linoleum floor vibrated under her feet and it had nothing to do with any alcohol this time. Car headlights swept through the window, tires crunching as the vehicle pulled into the driveway.

Rafe frowned. "Who would be coming here at midnight?"

Penny looked down and away quickly. Bob clapped his son on the shoulder, an apology already stamped all over his face.

Penny covered Sarah's hand and patted. "Your grandmother is here, honey."

Rafe jerked away from his father, anger radiating off him in waves. Sarah shot to her feet, jostling the table. She grabbed the edge to keep from swaying. The stack of textbooks slid to the side, spreading tourism flyers about Los Angeles across.

Tears stung her eyes over how the whole evening had fallen apart, but she blinked them back. She busied herself with gathering up a couple of maps of LA while she blinked away the moisture. The last thing she needed was for Rafe to get more upset and no doubt, if he saw her crying, he would grow angrier. God, she wanted to drop-kick that little Jason or whoever was responsible for spiking the punch.

Bob opened the squeaky screen door just as her grandmother stepped inside. Grandma Kat had passed down her red hair—and her temper—to Sarah. From the look of her grandma's tightly pressed lips, the temper was simmering close to the surface.

"Sarah," her grandmother said tersely. "Time to go home."

"Rafe will take me." She stood her ground. Rafe might not be much like his family. But there was no mistaking Sarah was completely, through and through, a Richards.

Kathleen Richards's gaze zipped from her to her date then back to her again. "I think it's best that you come with me now."

"Someone spiked the punch at the prom," she said slowly, carefully. "He brought me straight here for coffee, like a responsible date."

Her grandmother brushed her feet on the doormat and walked farther into the room. "These people aren't your family or legal guardians, which is why they called me. Rafe should have brought you home. If you had nothing to hide, there wouldn't have been a problem, now would there?"

Her face burned with a flush of anger over her grandmother's refusal to believe her. "I'm a senior in high school, only a month away from graduating and being on my own."

"Almost on your own. But not quite." She waved a hand toward the door. "Sarah, get in the car."

Rafe stood tall and tense, his jaw tight as he faced her grandmother, strongly but respectfully. "Ma'am, I am sorry. You trusted me with your granddaughter and I let you down."

"Thank you for the apology," Kathleen answered, some of the starch going out of her spine. And then her eyes narrowed. "Young man, one of the best things in life a person can learn is when you're in over your head. Tonight, you were in over your head with Sarah. Think about it. Now if you'll excuse me, Sarah should be at home, with her family."

Her grandmother wrapped an arm around her shoulders and steered her toward the door. Sarah looked back at Rafe, pleading with her eyes. Their prom night couldn't end this way. He should charge in, claim her, declare they were a couple. They were going to leave together after graduation.

But he didn't say a word. He didn't even walk with her to the car. As she sat in the front seat of her grandmother's old boat-sized sedan, she watched in the rearview mirror as Rafe simply closed the front door without so much as a glance of regret her way.

She scraped a sliding spaghetti strap back up and tried not to think about how she'd almost tossed away her clothes and her virginity tonight. She'd been ready to give him everything, her body, her heart, her future. She'd been so certain he cared about her as much as she loved him when he didn't take advantage of her offer on Busted Bluff.

But now she wondered if he'd stopped for another reason. Her mind skated back to those flyers and maps of Los Angeles mixed in with his textbooks. She'd assumed it must be for a school project, but now she wondered if he'd been making plans to go already, without even talking to her. He had to know a big city like that would be dead last on her list. She couldn't ignore the niggling sense that he was holding back in their relationship so he would have fewer regrets after graduation when he left town…

Without her.

COMING NEXT MONTH

Available May 10, 2011

HDCNM0411

REQUEST YOUR FREE BOOKS!
2 FREE NOVELS PLUS 2 FREE GIFTS!

ALWAYS POWERFUL, PASSIONATE AND PROVOCATIVE

YES! Please send me 2 FREE Harlequin Desire® novels and my 2 FREE gifts (gifts are worth about $10). After receiving them, if I don't wish to receive any more books, I can return the shipping statement marked "cancel." If I don't cancel, I will receive 6 brand-new novels every month and be billed just $4.05 per book in the U.S. or $4.74 per book in Canada. That's a saving of at least 15% off the cover price! It's quite a bargain! Shipping and handling is just 50¢ per book in the U.S. and 75¢ per book in Canada.* I understand that accepting the 2 free books and gifts places me under no obligation to buy anything. I can always return a shipment and cancel at any time. Even if I never buy another book, the two free books and gifts are mine to keep forever.

225/326 SDN FC65

Name _____ (PLEASE PRINT)

Address _____ Apt. #

City _____ State/Prov. _____ Zip/Postal Code

Signature (if under 18, a parent or guardian must sign)

Mail to the **Reader Service:**
IN U.S.A.: P.O. Box 1867, Buffalo, NY 14240-1867
IN CANADA: P.O. Box 609, Fort Erie, Ontario L2A 5X3

Not valid for current subscribers to Harlequin Desire books.

Want to try two free books from another line?
Call 1-800-873-8635 or visit www.ReaderService.com.

* Terms and prices subject to change without notice. Prices do not include applicable taxes. Sales tax applicable in N.Y. Canadian residents will be charged applicable taxes. Offer not valid in Quebec. This offer is limited to one order per household. All orders subject to credit approval. Credit or debit balances in a customer's account(s) may be offset by any other outstanding balance owed by or to the customer. Please allow 4 to 6 weeks for delivery. Offer available while quantities last.

Your Privacy—The Reader Service is committed to protecting your privacy. Our Privacy Policy is available online at www.ReaderService.com or upon request from the Reader Service.

We make a portion of our mailing list available to reputable third parties that offer products we believe may interest you. If you prefer that we not exchange your name with third parties, or if you wish to clarify or modify your communication preferences, please visit us at www.ReaderService.com/consumerchoice or write to us at Reader Service Preference Service, P.O. Box 9062, Buffalo, NY 14269. Include your complete name and address.

HDES11

*With an evil force hell-bent on destruction,
two enemies must unite to find a truth that turns
all-too-personal when passions collide.*

*Enjoy a sneak peek in Jenna Kernan's next installment
in her original* TRACKER *series, GHOST STALKER,
available in May, only from Harlequin Nocturne.*

"Who are you?" he snarled.

Jessie lifted her chin. "Your better."

His smile was cold. "Such arrogance could only come from a Niyanoka."

She nodded. "Why are you here?"

"I don't know." He glanced about her room. "I asked the birds to take me to a healer."

"And they have done so. Is that *all* you asked?"

"No. To lead them away from my friends." His eyes fluttered and she saw them roll over white.

Jessie straightened, preparing to flee, but he roused himself and mastered the momentary weakness. His eyes snapped open, locking on her.

Her heart hammered as she inched back.

"Lead who away?" she whispered, suddenly afraid of the answer.

"The ghosts. Nagi sent them to attack me so I would bring them to her."

The wolf must be deranged because Nagi did not send ghosts to attack living creatures. He captured the evil ones after their death if they refused to walk the Way of Souls, forcing them to face judgment.

"Her? The healer you seek is also female?"

"Michaela. She's Niyanoka, like you. The last Seer of Souls and Nagi wants her dead."

Jessie fell back to her seat on the carpet as the possibility of this ricocheted in her brain. Could it be true?

"Why should I believe you?" But she knew why. His black aura, the part that said he had been touched by death. Only a ghost could do that. But it made no sense.

Why would Nagi hunt one of her people and why would a Skinwalker want to protect her? She had been trained from birth to hate the Skinwalkers, to consider them a threat.

His intent blue eyes pinned her. Jessie felt her mouth go dry as she considered the impossible. Could the trickster be speaking the truth? Great Mystery, what evil was this?

She stared in astonishment. There was only one way to find her answers. But she had never even met a Skinwalker before and so did not even know if they dreamed.

But if he dreamed, she would have her chance to learn the truth.

Look for GHOST STALKER by Jenna Kernan, available May only from Harlequin Nocturne, wherever books and ebooks are sold.